Bark!
The Herald
Angels Sing

The Dogfather · Book Eight

roxanne st. claire

Bark! The Herald Angels Sing
THE DOGFATHER BOOK EIGHT
Copyright © 2018 Roxanne St. Claire

This novel is a work of fiction. Any references to historical events, real people, or real locales are used fictitiously. Other names, characters, places, and incidents are the product of the author's imagination, and any resemblance to actual events or locales or persons, living or dead, is coincidental.

All rights to reproduction of this work are reserved. No part of this publication may be reproduced, stored in or introduced into a retrieval system, or transmitted, in any form, or by any means (electronic, mechanical, photocopying, recording, or otherwise) without prior written permission from the copyright owner. Thank you for respecting the copyright. For permission or information on foreign, audio, or other rights, contact the author, roxanne@roxannestclaire.com

978-0-9993621-7-4 – ebook
978-0-9993621-8-1 – print

COVER ART: Keri Knutson (designer)
and Dawn C. Whitty (photographer)
INTERIOR FORMATTING: Author EMS

Critical Reviews of
Roxanne St. Claire Novels

"St. Claire, as always, brings a scorching tear-up-the-sheets romance combined with a great story: dealing with real issues starring memorable characters in vivid scenes."

— *Romantic Times Magazine*

"Non-stop action, sweet and sexy romance, lively characters, and a celebration of family and forgiveness."

— *Publishers Weekly*

"Plenty of heat, humor, and heart!"

— *USA Today's Happy Ever After blog*

"It's safe to say I will try any novel with St. Claire's name on it."

— *www.smartbitchestrashybooks.com*

"The writing was perfectly on point as always and the pace of the story was flawless. But be forewarned that you will laugh, cry, and sigh with happiness. I sure did."

— *www.harlequinjunkies.com*

"The Barefoot Bay series is an all-around knockout, soul-satisfying read. Roxanne St. Claire writes with warmth and heart and the community she's built at Barefoot Bay is one I want to visit again and again."

— *Mariah Stewart, New York Times bestselling author*

"This book stayed with me long after I put it down."

— *All About Romance*

Don't miss a single book in The Dogfather Series!

Available now
Sit…Stay…Beg (Book 1)
New Leash on Life (Book 2)
Leader of the Pack (Book 3)
Santa Paws is Coming to Town (Book 4 – a Holiday novella)
Bad to the Bone (Book 5)
Ruff Around the Edges (Book 6)
Double Dog Dare (Book 7)
Bark! The Herald Angels Sing (Book 8 – a Holiday novella)

Coming soon
Old Dog New Tricks (Book 9)

Find information and buy links for all these books here:
www.roxannestclaire.com/dogfather-series

And yes, there will be more. For a complete list, buy links, and reading order of *all* my books, visit www.roxannestclaire.com. Be sure to sign up for my newsletter on my website to find out when the next book is released! And join the private Dogfather Facebook group for inside info on all the books and characters, sneak peeks, and a place to share the love of tails and tales!

www.facebook.com/groups/roxannestclairereaders/

Bark!
The Herald
Angels Sing

Chapter One

"Where is everyone?" Pru plodded through the empty house, dismayed to find every room deadly quiet. No laughter, no talking, and, weirdest of all, no barking.

"In the living room."

Finally. Gramma Finnie's voice through the hall was music to Pru's ears, making her stride faster toward the living room to find her great-grandmother settled on a sofa, surrounded by red, green, and gold wrapping paper and dozens of holiday-styled ribbons.

"Oh no ye don't, child." Gramma Finnie leaned over the table and made a feeble attempt to use her narrow frame to cover a few of the items laid out for wrapping. "You can't come in here when this elf is working."

Pru stifled a laugh and pretended to cover her eyes after taking a peek. "Just hide the makeup bag and sparkly cell phone case and, oh please, God, tell me those Shopkins are for seven-year-old Christian and not fourteen-year-old me."

Gramma Finnie's deep-frown wrinkles grew even deeper. And frownier. "The makeup bag is for your mother, the cell phone case for your aunt Darcy, and…you don't collect those crazy critters anymore?"

Pru heaved the most dramatic sigh of pure discontent she had in her, and after one semester in ninth grade, where dramatic sighs were as common as black eyeliner and subtweets, she could deliver an Oscar-worthy exhale.

It must have worked, because Gramma backed off from her loot, her blue eyes pinned on Pru with intensity. "That doesn't sound like Christmas cheer."

"Oh, it's Christmas? That's right. Tomorrow's Christmas Eve, not that anyone cares around here."

Gramma's tiny jaw dropped open. "Prudence Anne Kilcannon." She rolled Pru's given name with a little thicker brogue than usual, a surefire way to know this mother of two, grandmother of ten, and great-grandmother of three-and-counting wasn't at all pleased. "What would make you say such a thing?"

Pru considered how much she should confide. Gramma Finnie might be eighty-seven and hold the unrivaled status of Pru's favorite person on the face of the earth, not counting Mom, but the elderly matriarch of the Kilcannon clan never tolerated disrespect or an unkind word about a single member of her brood.

"Nothing," she murmured. At Gramma's doubtful look, she added, "I just combed this whole house, and not a creature is stirring," Pru explained. "Not even a *dog*. Where *is* everyone?" And by *everyone*, she meant her mother.

"Out and about and doing the things that make Waterford Farm the best canine training and rescue facility in the world," she said brightly.

"On Christmas Eve eve?"

"Oh, they're all taking next week off for your mother's wedding, so everyone's squeezing in last-minute things."

Pru swallowed at the mention of the very thing that had her feeling squirrelly today. "Mmm," she said, hoping that didn't give anything away. "Like what?"

"My son, who really should run for mayor of Bitter Bark, had a holiday gathering of the Cultural Advisory Committee in town, so Rusty must be in the kennels for company."

"Isn't Linda May Dunlap on that committee?" She waggled her brows. "I still think Grandpa kind of likes her."

Gramma tsked. "I don't know, and I promised your father I wouldn't partake in the meddling of his personal life that his own children and grandchildren are merrily betting on. He's still not ready, nor should he be rushed. If and when the right lady friend comes along, he'll know it."

Pru shrugged. "Mom thought it would be nice for him to have a date for the wedding." And speaking of her mother… "Where's everyone else?"

"Darcy's swamped with last-minute holiday haircuts today, so Waterford's dog grooming studio is packed. All of your uncles are working with trainers to finish this group and send them home for the holidays. Your uncle Aidan and soon-to-be aunt Beck have flown that little Chihuahua to a forever home in Savannah and won't be back until tomorrow."

"Rudolf?" The thought of the rescue that had recently come to Waterford—and, of course, got named for the season—made her smile. "I loved that dog."

"Aye, he's a gem. Someone is going to have a good Christmas when they find that treasure under the tree."

Pru nodded, but her mind went back to her original problem, because Gramma actually hadn't solved it with her long explanation of everyone's whereabouts. "But where's Mom? She isn't in the vet office, and she's usually here on Fridays. And Trace wasn't training the service dogs."

"Are you always going to call him Trace?" Gramma asked. "Because on December thirtieth, he's officially your dad."

"He's been officially my dad for fourteen years, Gramma, only we didn't know it," Pru reminded her. "And I tried calling him Dad after they got engaged. Sounded weird. He's just Trace. But he's not here, either. Or Meatball, but he's probably wherever Trace is."

"Meatball's in the kennels. Molly and Trace went to meet with the wedding planner." Gramma mumbled the words and noisily shook out some tissue paper in a lousy effort to cover up what she was saying.

But Pru heard, and hurt. Of course Mom was with the wedding planner—the *professional* wedding planner. Funny, Pru never dreamed of getting jealous about the appearance of a man—her missing father— who suddenly took her immediate family from a happy twosome to an even happier family of three. But that darn Cassie St. Croix had to show up, and now the green-eyed monster had a solid hold of Pru.

Even the wedding planner's name irritated Pru, and the amount of time she spent with Mom was literally ridiculous. All Mom ever talked about was Cassie.

Cassie wants to do this with the candles, and *Cassie thinks white poinsettias are better than red*, and *Cassie said we should—*

"Pru?"

She shook off the thoughts and looked at Gramma, who was eyeing her with those wise, discerning Irish eyes blurred by bifocals and age, but they still never missed a thing. "Tell me your troubles, wee one." She patted the sofa in invitation. "Unless you're feeling too *grown-up* to be called wee."

If she were a *grown-up*, she'd be part of the wedding planning. Heck, she'd *be* the wedding planner. Instead, she was treated like the flower girl instead of the maid of honor.

Gramma rubbed the cushion with one of her knotted, spotted but oh-so-soft hands. "Come along, lass."

Pru couldn't resist the invitation to cozy up to the tiny woman who smelled like talcum powder and had a freakish knowledge of clever Irish sayings that always made things better. Rounding the coffee table, Pru glanced at the array of gifts, her attention slipping to the little purple Shopkins box.

"I do still kind of like them," she admitted with a dry laugh.

Gramma just smiled. "Good. I'll put one in the makeup bag that really is for you but is supposed to be a surprise."

Pru settled on the sofa and flipped up the half-open lid of Gramma's laptop, which rested on the next cushion. "Did you finish your Christmas blog?"

The older woman lifted a slender shoulder covered, as always, in a soft, silky cardigan. "I have what is apparently called writer's block. Nothing inspires me this Christmas."

"How is that possible?" Pru asked. "Just look around this room."

They both did, taking in the insane amount of holiday decorations draped throughout the formal living room of the big farmhouse. The space was out of the way of the main traffic and largely ignored unless the entire family had converged for Wednesday or Sunday dinner, and someone needed a quiet space to talk or rock a baby.

But after Thanksgiving, this high-ceilinged formal living space became Christmas Central for the ever-growing Kilcannon family and friends. The feature, of course, was a ten-foot live tree, cut from Waterford's woods, laden with ornaments that dated back nearly sixty years, or more if you added in Gramma's crystal snowflakes from Ireland. Lights sparkled on the tree and around the windows, ribbons twirled the fireplace columns, and every surface was adorned with an angel, Santa, or a little drummer boy.

The Nativity set had a place of honor on a Victorian chocolate table that had belonged to one of Pru's great-great-grandmothers from County Waterford, where her grandpa Seamus had lived before he and Gramma bought these hundred acres and named the homestead after that very place.

They'd raised Pru's grandfather, Daniel, and his sister, Colleen, in this house until Grandpa married Grannie Annie, and then the next generation of Kilcannons raised their six Kilcannon kids in this house, including Molly, Pru's mother.

Along the mantel, there were so many stockings,

they barely fit. Seventeen in all, Pru knew, because she'd hung every one herself, all with names hand-stitched by Gramma.

"So much Christmas history in this room," Pru mused. "That alone should inspire you."

Gramma gave a little sniff and shudder. "Sixty-four Christmases here. Or five. I've lost count."

Oh, that didn't sound at all like Gramma. "What's wrong?" Pru asked, leaning closer.

"Oh no." Two gray eyebrows rose. "You first. What's troubling *you*?"

Pru flicked her wrist to dismiss the inquiry. "Oh, you know, just the 'will Santa come or not?' blues."

Gramma snorted at the obvious lie. "He came early and filled up this table."

Pru lifted the makeup bag that would soon be hers, remembering she and Mom had seen it in La Parisienne when they were shopping for Darcy's gift last weekend. Pru loved the glitter that spelled out Good Vibes and had no doubt Mom had gone back in and bought it for her. So why wasn't Mom wrapping it?

Because she was with Cassie St. Croix. At the rise of bitter jealousy, she looked away, not wanting to tell even Gramma Finnie, who knew her inner soul what she was feeling.

Then one slightly crooked finger reached over and touched her chin, turning Pru's face until their gazes met. "I'll go first, then, and maybe you'll tell me the truth."

Pru stayed silent, staring at Gramma Finnie.

"I'm dying," Gramma confessed in a hush voice.

Pru blinked, drew back, and blinked again, and then she felt the blood drain from her head so fast, it left her a little dizzy. She could handle a lot of things—even this wedding—but not…that. Never that. Not yet. Not…*no*.

"Are you sick?" Pru barely whispered the question, it scared her so much.

"I'm healthy as a horse."

Pru searched her face, not finding a clue on the network of familiar wrinkles. "Then why are you…"

"I'm dyin' of *boredom*, child."

"Oh." Relief rocked her down to her toes. It was Gramma being Gramma. Not serious. "Then you need to do something."

"Can't. I'm too old." The response was simple and pure and a little heartbreaking. Pru had never, not once, heard Gramma complain about her age. About anything, to be fair. She was optimistic, but grounded, and if she had the aches and pains that plagued most eight-seven-year-olds, no one knew it. Even Pru, and they told each other everything.

"You're not that…" At Gramma's notched brow, Pru's words trailed off. Okay, she was old. "But you said you're healthy," she finished.

"Mmm." She nodded and patted her soft white hair. "Fit as a fiddle."

Thank God. "And I know I've heard you say 'the older the fiddle, the sweeter the tune,'" Pru reminded her gently. "In fact, you cross-stitched that on a wall hanging for one of your church friends' birthday."

"Ruth Blair." Gramma pursed her lips. "She died last June." At Pru's incredulous look, she laughed. "She was near a hundred, though."

"So you have plenty of time," Pru insisted, as much to comfort herself as this woman who made the "great" before grandma seem like the world's biggest understatement. Gramma Finnie was so far beyond great, it defied description.

"That's all I've got, child," she said with uncharacteristic sadness. "Time. Time to think about the past, which is what old people do, and hope there's a future, which will be brief no matter what happens during it, and live in a present that is as dull as dirt."

Pru's jaw literally fell so hard it almost hit her chest. "Dull? How can you even say that? You are the glue that holds us together, the heart of this family, the keeper of memories, the speaker of sayings, and the best storyteller in the world. Plus, Gramma, you have actual followers on your blog. Real people who care about what you think. They write to you and tell you that you inspired them or made them shed a tear. What on earth could be more useful than all that?"

It was Gramma Finnie's turn to flick a dismissive wrist. "It's all the same. Every day. I never go anywhere anymore. Never do anything but church. Why, child, there was a time when I lived for the next adventure around the corner."

Pru searched her face, scouring the crinkled cheeks and thin lips and seeing nothing but honesty in her faded blue eyes. "Then get *un*bored, Gramma Finnie," she said. "You'd be the first to tell me to that problems need fixin', not fumin'. Or some such thing."

She shook her old white head. "As if it would be that easy." She snorted. "They rarely let me drive, you know, not even to choir on Friday nights, like I used to."

Pru knew who *they* were—her mother, Trace, all four of her uncles, and, of course, Gramma's son, their patriarch, Grandpa Daniel Kilcannon.

"They don't let me drive, either," Pru said.

"You're fourteen and have no license."

Pru rolled her eyes. "I've been driving that Jeep around Waterford since I was eleven," she said. "But every time Uncle Garrett catches me, he gets so mad."

"And every time I even look at the keys to my car, someone swoops them out of my hand and offers to take me wherever I need taken."

"So you're too old and I'm too young for anything *fun.*"

"'Tis our lot in this life, it seems. So, enough about me. What has you fretting, child?" Gramma squeezed her hand. "Or is there a lad on your mind? A dustup with your lassies?"

She shook her head and glanced at the doorway, wanting complete privacy before she confided, which, of course she would. "It's the wedding," she finally admitted.

"Your mother and Trace's wedding?" Gramma seemed shocked. "You're not happy your birth parents have found each other and are marryin'? Why, it's one of the Dogfather's greatest success stories."

Pru smiled, acknowledging the fact that her grandfather had earned a nickname for pulling strings like the classic Godfather—but the strings he pulled invariably led to love. Six times he'd succeeded now, somehow managing to help all his kids find love. In the case of Pru's mother, Molly, he'd managed to reunite a single mom with the man who'd fathered her child and disappeared for fourteen years. And none of them had ever been happier.

"Of course I'm glad they found each other," Pru said. "I love Trace, and we're all a really good little family."

"But you're feeling left out?" she guessed. "Are they in a...oh, what does Darcy call it when she wants to hide away with her handsome landlord?"

"Love bubble," Pru supplied with a laugh, grateful that Gramma wasn't too old to use the many phrases she hears from the young people around her. "No, they don't go into a love bubble at home. They're really cool about that, which is probably why they haven't had a chance to do what needs to be done to give me a baby sister or brother, if you catch my drift."

"Drift caught," Gramma assured her. "But then what ails you, child?"

"It's not the marriage, it's the *wedding*," she repeated with more emphasis. "I've been excluded from it. *Me*. The person they call General Pru who is the most masterful list maker and task planner anyone would ever meet. They hired that stupid, overpriced, head-full-of-dumb ideas *wedding planner*."

Gramma inched back. "I had no idea you were feeling that way."

"So don't tell my mom," Pru said. "Please, whatever you do, don't tell my mom."

"Don't tell me *what*?"

Pru whipped around at the sound of a familiar voice. "Mom!" It was only a glimpse, only a millisecond, but Pru saw the instant flash of hurt in her mother's eyes.

Oh man. How much of that had she heard?

Chapter Two

S he hated the wedding planner?

Every protective, nurturing, maternal instinct in Molly—and there were many—stood up, brushed off, and began to search for a way to fix this problem.

"Were you listening?" Pru had a rare guilty look in her hazel eyes, and some color drained from her creamy skin, leaving one little blotch of red where a pimple plagued her. Molly even wanted to get rid of that. Anything to make her precious, sweet girl completely content.

She hates the wedding planner? How could Molly not know that? Because Pru was dear and considerate and unlike every other teenager on earth. Yes, many moms said that about their kids, but in Pru's case, it was true.

"Of course I wasn't listening," Molly denied easily, because she hadn't intentionally eavesdropped on the conversation. She'd merely taken off her boots in the kitchen and walked back here in silent, stocking feet and *heard*. "Now what can't you tell me?"

Of course she knew, but she wanted Pru to confide in her.

Pru's glance at Gramma would be surreptitious enough to miss...if Molly wasn't completely and utterly in tune with this girl she'd given birth to and raised as a single mother.

"Don't you be worrying about anything, lass." Gramma spread her aging hands wide over the table full of gifts. "Or lookin' at your pressies."

Except everything on that table was a gift Molly had asked Gramma to wrap for her because of the meeting with Cassie. Molly barely glanced at them, her mind whirring for an answer to solve Pru's problem.

What was it her own mother had said a million times? *You're only as happy as your least-happy child.* And this child, her only child, was not happy.

"So how was the meeting with the wedding planner?" Pru asked with a forced cheerfulness that twisted Molly's gut.

The wedding planner...that Pru hated. Which was such a shame, because Cassie was an absolute doll with fantastic ideas. "Really good," she said.

Pru kept her fake smile in place as long as she could, then averted her eyes, making Molly swallow hard. And then she caught Gramma secretly giving Pru's hand a squeeze of support. Oh God. That was Molly's job. And so was wrapping these gifts. And being available to her daughter the day before Christmas Eve. Mom guilt crawled up her chest.

Gramma cleared her throat and leaned closer, no doubt picking up every nuance of the dynamics in the room, as she always did. "What did your girl think of your plan to have the wedding party come down two by two instead of one at a time?"

Molly clasped her hands together, remembering the idea. "Oh, wait until you hear what she came up with to make that even better."

Pru lifted some colorful paper and a package of Matchbox cars for Christian, slipping to her knees to start wrapping without even looking at Molly.

"What is it?" Gramma asked, putting a hand on Pru's shoulder as if she wanted to offer the same comfort that Molly did.

"Well, I told her that all my brothers and my sister had fallen in love in the last year and a half, thanks to my dad. And a few amazing dogs," she added on a laugh.

"He still denies Darcy and Josh," Pru said, giving Molly some measure of relief that at least she was still talking to her.

"Well, you can't deny the dogs," Molly said. "And Cassie loved the idea of our attendants coming down the aisle as couples—"

"My idea," Pru muttered.

Molly's heart dropped. "Yes, it was."

"Along with Meatball being Trace's best man-dog."

Molly sighed. "Yes, also your idea, Pru. In fact, when I told her these ideas *of yours*, she loved them all." Okay...not exactly how the conversation had unfolded, but if it made Pru feel better, what difference did it make?

"She did?"

Encouraged, Molly dropped down on the chair next to her to tell them both the new plan. "She thinks the dogs should come in, too, right down the aisle between each groomsman and bridesmaid. So Andi and Liam will have Jag, and Shane and Chloe will have Ruby, Garrett and Jessie will have Lola, and so on."

Gramma gave a hoot. "And Darcy and Josh have two, and Aidan and Beck have Ruff, who is nine dogs in one."

Molly laughed. "Ruff will be fine, since he's been training to be a therapy dog for Beck's uncle. And, yes, Darcy and Josh will have Kookie and Stella. The church is cool with it, and since the reception is here, we can put them all in the kennels if things get out of control, but we do have a few dog trainers on hand, so..." She eyed Pru, who was even more industrious than usual in her wrapping job. "So, it'll be fun," she finished. "Don't you think, Pru?"

"Oh yeah. And Gramma and I will walk down the aisle alone? The only 'couple' without a dog?"

Dang it. She hadn't even thought about the maid and matron of honor.

"It's okay, Mom," Pru said before Molly could answer. "Like we've always said, I'll need to snag Meatball during the ceremony. I mean, I have to have *something* to do as maid of honor."

Ouch.

"You gave your mother that beautiful bridal shower," Gramma Finnie reminded her gently. "'Tis the most important job you have, lass."

"But..." Pru pushed some of her long dark hair over her shoulder. "Yeah." Her voice was soft, and it made Molly ache some more.

What else could Pru do? And then she remembered one other little item Cassie had mentioned, but it had seemed unimportant at the time—a minor task that would essentially take care of itself while Molly was dressing.

But maybe she could build it up a bit.

"Well, there is one other kind of critical part of a wedding, and it is entirely up to the maid of honor to plan and execute." Was that true? Well, it was now.

Finally, Pru met her gaze with genuine interest. "There is?"

"You, my sweet little maid of honor," Molly said, tapping her daughter's nose, "are in charge of the somethings."

"The what?"

"The somethings," Molly said. "Old, new, borrowed, and blue."

All that interest disappeared. "You have them all," Pru said. "New dress, old Claddagh ring that belonged to Grannie Annie." She pointed to the gold band Molly now wore on her left hand that would be turned after she married Trace. "You're borrowing Chloe's veil, and you're wearing that snazzy blue thong we got at Victoria's Secret."

"A thong on your wedding day?" Gramma tsked but added a sly smile. "And here I thought the garter was scandalous."

Molly laughed, but Pru shook her head.

"I got all the somethings covered a long time ago, Mom. Just like I thought of the dogs. And the Christmas sleigh to take you to the church," she added with a little uncharacteristic edge in her voice.

"Pru." Molly closed her eyes, ready to reprimand her for the tone, but forced herself to step into Pru's shoes, which would be easy since they wore the same size now. She had to remember Pru wasn't a little girl, and she was a big part of this wedding. The reason, really, it was happening. Had Pru not been conceived on a snowy night all those years ago, would she and Trace have ever reunited and fallen in love? Unlikely. So, she wanted Pru to dance and celebrate and be part of the event, not plan it.

But this was Pru, and planning was her *thing*.

"There is so much more to the somethings than merely grabbing certain items when you get dressed," Molly said, hoping she could figure out what that *much more* might be.

"There is?" Pru asked, glancing at Gramma Finnie. "Did you know that?"

"Aye." Gramma nodded, and the glimmer in her eye told Molly the older woman knew exactly what she was up to.

"So much more," Molly added.

"Like what?" Pru asked.

"Like…" Molly rooted around for something to make the somethings seem more important than a throwaway tradition. "They have to be…" *Help me out here, Gramma.*

"A surprise," Gramma interjected.

"Oh, yes," Molly agreed, sending a silent flash of gratitude with her eyes. "A surprise. To me, on the morning of the wedding. And only you can know what they are. Well, you and Gramma, since you're both the 'of honors' in this one."

Pru frowned. "I don't remember reading any of that in the wedding books I studied."

Oh. She'd studied wedding books. Of course she had. This was Prudence Kilcannon, industrious planner of all things.

"The surprise part is an Irish tradition," Gramma announced with so much certainty that Molly could have kissed her parchment-soft cheek. "You know what they say?"

"No." Pru wasn't quite buying this.

"Well, the saying goes…" Gramma took a slow, deep breath. "'Shock the bride with old, new, borrowed, and blue…'" She hesitated enough for Molly to know this was no Irish proverb like the ones she trotted out for every occasion. This was a stone-cold ad lib with a brogue.

"And?" Pru prodded, with enough doubt that it was obvious she suspected the same.

"'And she'll be favored…with not one child but two.'"

Whoa. Molly's eyes widened. Maybe Gramma had gone too far in this assist. "Oh, I don't think that's what—"

"Two?" Pru straightened like the four-star general they teased her about being. "Then this *is* the most important job of the whole event." Her eyes glistened. "I do want a little sister, Mom."

"Pru, we can't…we don't…" How could she tell her that that little sibling was not happening, and not for lack of trying?

"Mom, we all know you want another baby." Pru reached out, her hand warm on Molly's arm.

Molly managed a shrug. "It's not up to me. I'll let the man upstairs figure that out."

But Gramma and Pru were beaming at each other now, like Gramma hadn't just made up that silly poem on the spot.

Didn't she?

18

Pru leaned back and rubbed her hands gleefully. "Oh, we have got to get to work on this and fast! Christmas Eve is tomorrow, and then it's Christmas, and nothing is open the following week, and then it's the wedding."

"Then what are we waitin' for, lass? Let's get to thinkin' and doin' the somethings."

Pru showed off a mouthful of braces, complete with red and green bands, and the smile shot right to Molly's heart.

"Oh, the somethings are going to blow your socks off, Mom."

"Or your thong, as the case may be," Gramma deadpanned with a rise of her white brows.

They burst into laughter that came right from their bellies. Oh yes. Molly was only as happy as her least-happy child, and the only one she had—for now, at least—looked very, very happy.

"Mom, can I stay at Waterford tonight?" Pru asked.

Molly's laugh faded. "On Christmas Eve eve? We were going to have pizza night and help Trace wrap his Kilcannon presents."

"You and Trace have pizza night and wrap." Pru leaned into her great-grandmother with that silent conspiratorial exchange Molly knew so well from these two. "I want to stay here so Gramma and I can get an early start tomorrow on the somethings."

"All right." Plus, she wouldn't mind the alone time at home in case there was some truth to Gramma's fake poem. "But tomorrow is Christmas Eve, so—"

"So we'll all be in this house at five o'clock, like every other Christmas Eve," Pru said. "Gramma will light the lantern for the window, and we'll exchange some early gifts and then go to Midnight Mass. But what we do before that is our business."

"But—"

"Mom, please? Can just this one thing for your wedding be all mine?"

If that made her happy, even if it meant giving up the day tomorrow, then Molly would, of course, agree. When she nodded, Pru and Gramma shared another glance that Molly should have been able to interpret, but suspected it was another secret, silent message between great-grandmother and great-granddaughter.

"I already have a plan," Pru whispered.

"You're in charge," Molly said, pushing up.

"You have to promise to let us handle it completely," Pru said. "And not to worry, ask questions, or poke around where you aren't supposed to."

Molly crossed her heart. "I promise." Leaning over, she gave each of them a kiss on their heads, quite satisfied that she'd averted a prewedding disaster and, most important, made her daughter happy again.

Chapter Three

"Can I make my mother and grand-daughter a fire before I leave?" Grandpa poked his head into Gramma's upstairs living area where Pru had set up Somethings Central after dinner that night. "And may I offer a friendly Irish setter to join you?"

Without invitation, Rusty came trotting into the room, somehow avoiding the papers and notes Pru had spread on the floor.

"My, don't you cut a fine figure in your fancy clothes, lad?" Gramma slowed the rock of her chair as she looked her son up and down. He did look pretty dressed up in a pullover sweater and slacks he usually wore to church. "Who's the lucky lady?"

He narrowed eyes exactly the same blue as his mother's. "Finola Brennan Kilcannon. We had a deal that you were on my side in this ridiculous family campaign."

She laughed. "You sound like your father when you call me that."

"Then maybe you'll listen to me and put that subject to bed."

"Well. You look dressed enough to put *something* to bed," she muttered under her breath.

Pru snorted at a comment that only Gramma Finnie could get away with, but Grandpa closed his eyes and shook his head.

"I'm going to Bella Peterson's Christmas party."

"Then you'll be coming home covered in cat hair," Pru said.

"Or the cat lady's long blonde hair," Gramma added.

He shot her a look, but then surveyed the room, and Pru looked up to study him. Her grandfather was, what, sixty? He certainly wasn't decrepit, but he sure seemed way too old to date, in Pru's eyes.

But her aunts, uncles, and parents didn't agree. All they ever did was try to set him up, either to make him happy—though he seemed pretty happy to Pru—or to return the favor for what he'd done for all of them.

All along, Grandpa insisted he wasn't ready to date anyone, and Pru understood that. Grannie Annie had died only four years ago, from a heart attack that no one ever dreamed could happen, ripping the soul right out of the Kilcannon clan. Yes, her memory was fading in Pru's head, but it had to be strong for Grandpa.

"A man comes up here and kindly offers to make his two favorite ladies a fire on a chilly December night, and he gets teased and tortured by his own mother."

Pru stroked Rusty's soft red fur as the dog settled next to her, and Gramma resumed rocking with an apologetic smile. "We'll take that fire, lad, with gratitude."

He nodded, satisfied, and made his way across the room with a quick glance at Pru's notes and two tablets plus a laptop, all open to different sites about wedding traditions, Christmas nuptials, and creative somethings.

"What are you two concocting now?" he asked as he picked up some logs from the basket next to the fireplace.

"Oh, we're just—"

"It's a surprise," Pru interjected. "As many things at Christmas are, so don't look too closely."

"I get it." He made a show of covering the sides of his eyes while he knelt to kindle the fire. "I'm forever grateful I didn't know last year's big surprise, which turned out to be one of the best Christmases of my life."

Of all their lives, Pru thought, remembering the drama around little Jack Frost, the "missing" terrier. "Well, we don't have anything quite that big and dramatic this year," Pru said. "This Christmas is all about a wedding."

"Then why all the secrecy?" Grandpa asked, glancing over his shoulder at her.

"Just...because."

"Aye," Gramma said. "Just because." She knew why they were being secretive: If there was any need for Gramma and Pru to leave Waterford to get the perfect somethings, then Grandpa would offer to take them, and then Gramma Finnie wouldn't get a chance to leave and drive and feel young and alive again.

Her great-grandmother might think this whole thing was for Pru to get her wedding planning on, but there was another, equally important side bennie to

23

this project, which was giving Gramma Finnie a purpose and *fun*.

Because no one was dying of boredom, or anything else. Not if Pru had a say in things. But Grandpa was still waiting for an explanation, his silver-blue eyes leveled on Pru like a man who rarely took no for an answer.

"Because Christmas secrets are meant to stay secret, Grandpa," she told him, mustering all her General Pru authority.

But he lifted a brow. "You said *wedding* secrets."

Nope. Not happening. "So is it really a party, or is it a date with Bella?" Pru volleyed back.

That made him chuckle and turn back to the fire without answering, lighting some newspaper and stoking the flames. "I'm sure your mother, father, and the wedding planner know about these wedding surprises."

"Mom gave us the job, with me in charge."

"And if you don't mind, Prudence and I have work to do, lad. Unless you want to tell us about your *date* with Bella tonight."

"It's not a..." He blew out a breath and stood to leave. Behind his back, Pru gave a thumbs-up to Gramma Finnie, the world's greatest partner in crime.

"I won't be out late," Grandpa said. "But you two are home alone, so I'd appreciate it if you'd take Rusty out before bed just in case I don't make it home by eleven."

"Will do," Pru promised, adding a good rub to Rusty's belly, now exposed as he rolled onto his back next to her.

"Thank you." Grandpa bent over and kissed his mother's head and then turned, bent more, and kissed Pru's. "And whatever your surprise, I'm sure it will be wonderful."

"It will be," she agreed. If he'd ever leave and let them work. "And thanks for the fire, Grandpa."

He glanced around the little room, which was almost as well-decorated with holiday cheer as the living room two stories below. "It does complete the atmosphere. Good night, you two. Have fun."

"And you, lad," Gramma added with just enough of a tease in her brogue that Grandpa shot her one last look on the way out, making Pru giggle.

Pru had done a lot of laughing the last few hours, so pleased with this turn of events, and the smile didn't fade as she looked back at her laptop and skimmed the Pinterest page she'd opened about Irish wedding traditions.

"You know, there's a lot about horseshoes here, Gramma. I know it's not Christmasy, but could we scare up a horseshoe?"

Gramma looked up, her skin seeming to pale a little even in the warm firelight. "A horseshoe?" Her voice sounded strange.

Did she not know the significance? Pru gestured to the screen. "It says that there should be a horseshoe at every Irish wedding for good luck. Otherwise, the marriage won't last. Better not tell Shane and Chloe, Liam and Andi, or Garrett and Jessie. I don't remember any horseshoes at their weddings, do you?"

Pru looked up, surprised to see Gramma slowly pushing out of her rocker.

"Where are you going?"

"Back in time," she muttered. "Come, child. I have a perfect something old."

"You do?" Pru got up to follow Gramma to the open door that led to her bedroom, a sanctuary that was one of Pru's favorite spaces in the whole house, maybe all of Waterford Farm.

Situated at the corner of the third floor, this bedroom always had that faint scent of talcum, with the perfect amount of light either through the shutters or from the crystal lamps on either side of a lumpy double bed piled with pillows, all cross-stitched by Gramma over the years. The ancient white and brass bedframe was pressed into Pru's earliest memories.

Grandpa Seamus had died when Pru was a baby, and Gramma had moved back to Waterford Farm. With her mother studying and working for a degree in veterinary medicine, Pru had taken many naps on this bed, played peekaboo for hours, listened to a hundred stories, both real and fictional. Over the years, she'd forged a closeness with her sweet great-grandmother that probably shaped her as much as any relationship in her family.

Gramma pulled open her ancient wardrobe—a heavy, ornate piece of furniture that had come and gone and come back again in popularity. It was the type of thing that would be painted and "distressed" now, but this old maple wood had aged as gracefully as its owner.

Pru settled on the bed, watching as Gramma rooted through one of the drawers, then another, and finally pulled out a round, linen-covered box decorated with purple flowers embroidered all over it. For a long moment, she didn't speak but held the box with total reverence, running one finger over the top, settling it on the button nestled in the tufted fabric.

"It belonged to Mary Violet."

Pru frowned, digging back into those stories she'd heard in this room. Mary Violet? She'd never heard that name before. "Who was she?"

"My sister," Gramma whispered. "The most beautiful girl you'd ever lay your eyes on."

Pru sat up and seized this new piece of information. "You had a sister?" How on earth could she not know that? "A sister named Mary Violet?" How could Pru, the keeper of the family record, the person whose job it was to read every name in the Kilcannon family bible at baby Fiona's christening last month, *not* know this?

Granted, the family tree always leaned stronger toward the Kilcannon side, but Pru knew about the Brennans, from County Wexford on the southeast coast of Ireland. Knew they had a farm and that Gramma had three brothers—Patrick, Jack, and Edward—but a sister?

"To be fair, her name was Mary Violet, but we called her Vi."

"Vi." Pru breathed the single syllable, suddenly intrigued. "Tell me about her."

A little chill of anticipation crawled up Pru's spine. She loved nothing more than Gramma's stories, which had entertained and lulled her to sleep her entire life. Even if she'd told one a hundred times, the woman had the Irish gift of telling a story that always seemed to capture some deep human emotion.

And even the telling of it was an experience. Gramma's brogue grew thicker, her touch more tender, and the words she shared always transported Pru to another place and time.

But Mary Violet? Pru had never been transported to anywhere that long-lost relative was.

Gramma didn't say anything, still holding the box as her shoulders rose and fell with a sigh.

"Is that why there are violets on there?" Pru guessed.

"Mmm." She finally turned and joined Pru on the bed, laying the antique jewel box on the comforter between them. "'Tis why. I made it after…after…" She closed her eyes. "I made it to hold something dear."

"A horseshoe?" Pru guessed.

"But not any horseshoe. This one was special." The last word caught in her throat, making Pru lean closer. Gramma Finnie so rarely cried, it stunned her to think she might.

"But it's making you sad, Gramma. Maybe it's not right for something old."

Finally, Gramma lifted her eyes from the box. "'Tis where you're wrong, lass." Instead of sadness, there was a radiance to her look. "It was Christmastime of 1943, and the world was black with war. Not my world, mind you, and not my war. Down in County Wexford, it was white with a snowfall, and being Irish, we were spared what they were enduring in Britain and on the Continent."

Pru zipped through her last semester of European history, always attuned to the role of the Irish in any major event. "Ireland was neutral during that war," she said.

"Neutral?" Gramma let out a sarcastic choke as her

knotted fingers opened the box lid, revealing a bed of purple velvet. "Tell that to the thousands that sneaked off to join the war. Thousands of young men…"

Pru leaned over to get a better look in the box, seeing a long stickpin with a horseshoe in the middle and a bright green shamrock attached to one side. The other side appeared to be broken metal, where something had fallen off.

Gramma lifted the piece and placed it in her soft, pink palm. "Thousands of men and some women," she sighed. "Some fearless, some feckless, some mere lassies searchin' for an adventure. Aye." She nodded, and her eyes misted. "They went to war, too."

Chapter Four

County Wexford, Ireland, 1943

"Promise me, lass. Promise. Swear on our grandmother's grave, Finola Brennan. You will not tell a soul."

"I'll swear to no such thing, Vi." Finnie Brennan pulled her woolen collar tighter against the cold December air, squinting at her oldest sibling and only sister, who somehow looked fresh and alive no matter the predawn hour or icy warning of more snow.

Finnie had come to the barn to do her morning chores with nothing on her mind but the trip she'd make that day to John Brody's market to help Mammy pick parsnips and brussels sprouts for tomorrow night's Christmas Eve dinner. But when she turned the corner behind the hayloft, she came face-to-face with an equally shocked Mary Violet, all dressed and hitching up the cart to Alphonsus.

The old horse clomped his hoof at the sight of Finnie, or maybe because he was being called to duty before the sun.

"Where are you going?" Finnie insisted.

Vi's blue eyes—so dark you'd swear that's where she got her middle name that everyone used to address her—flashed in warning.

"Never you mind, Finnie." She looked around, a wee bit nervous. "Just don't tell anyone I've left. I'm beggin' ye."

"Are you coming back before breakfast?"

Violet didn't answer, giving Finnie a bit of hope for a real treat.

"Then can I have your biscuits?" If she didn't claim them now, little Jack would steal every last morsel on the table.

A smile threatened, but it was tempered by sadness. "They're yours, lass. All of them."

Oh, something was not right with the world if Vi wasn't going to at least save one biscuit for the bread pudding.

"Are you sure?" Finnie pressed, not wanting to get too certain of her good biscuit fortune.

Her sister's only answer was a sigh that slipped through perfectly shaped ruby lips. Aye, Mary Violet Brennan was the prettiest girl in the county, and that wasn't just Finnie's twelve-year-old eyes seeing it. At eighteen, Vi was near past marrying age for these parts of rural Ireland, and most every boy from Enniscorthy to the port had noticed that, not that she cared.

With cascading waves of hair the color of the mahogany dining table Mammy loved so much and perfect white teeth that reminded Finnie of the American movie stars they saw at the cinema house in town on Saturday mornings, Vi was a sight to behold.

And when she laughed, well, it was like the angels themselves burst into song.

But it wasn't her fine bones or sweet voice that made Mary Violet beautiful. 'Twas a heart so pure and giving, she likely had saints in heaven moving sideways to make room for her already. Vi was gentle and kind to every sick person, but somehow fearless and fierce, too.

After a year of making rounds with Dr. O'Connell, who tended to the country folk in these parts, Vi started working as a nurse at St. Aidan's Hospital off Market Square in Enniscorthy, and somehow that role fit her perfectly. It was like she had a halo atop her shiny hair.

But that halo would fall and choke her if Mammy and Da found their cart and best horse and the eldest Brennan all gone missing two days before Christmas.

"When will you be back?" Finnie asked.

"I won't be home today." There was a note in her voice, a little bittersweet, a little daring, that did something strange to Finnie's heart.

"But you're takin' the horse?"

"I'll leave the rig at Brody's in Carrig Hill and get a transport to Wexford."

"You're going clear out to Wexford?"

Vi shrugged off the question. "You and Edward can hike out later when you get the parsnips and bring the rig and Alphonsus home."

Did she really think her brother would be free to do that and not tend the poor freezing pigs? "And what'll I tell Mammy and Da?" Who'd surely strap Finnie raw if she went along with such a plan.

Vi narrowed her eyes to thin blue slits. "Tell them lives depend on it."

Lives? "Whose?"

"The men dyin' in the war, child. They need nurses in England. They're desperate for nurses in London, and I intend to be one."

London? Finnie almost fell over backward with each new bomb that fell on her exactly like they were falling in London. "'Tisn't safe!"

"Which is why they need nurses."

Finnie blinked and tried to understand this, but she couldn't think for the blood rushing in her head. "You can't go to London!" Her voice rose in panic. "How could you possibly get there?"

"A boat from Dublin, which I will get after I take one from Wexford Port. I've got it all planned."

"But...people are dyin' in London." She couldn't help the screech in her voice.

"Hush." Vi pulled her closer and put a hand over Finnie's mouth. "Donchya be trying to stop me, lass. Why do you think I have to go? There's need there."

"There's need here," Finnie shot back. "At the hospital and in the country. Folk need nurses here, but—"

"Timothy is there. He's written to me and asked me to come." A soft flush rose on her cheeks. So maybe Vi *did* care about one of those young suiters. But this wasn't just any boy from two farms over.

Timothy Donovan had "disappeared" almost two years ago. Even Finnie knew what that meant. Like thousands of other young Irishmen who couldn't stand Ireland's "neutrality" one more day, he'd gone to fight alongside the British. And *die* alongside the British.

"He's in the RAF," she whispered with an edge of

excitement to her voice. "The 184th Squadron in Kingsnorth."

Finnie shuddered, the words so foreign, yet vaguely familiar from newsreels and hearing her brothers whisper about it. Softly, so Da didn't hear. "And you're going there?"

"I can't, but he'll come to me in London, where I'll work. We're going to marry."

She'd truly lost all sense. "Da will never stand for you marryin' a soldier." She had heard her parents discuss this late at night when they thought she was asleep. Everyone knew. They knew where Timmy had gone and that it wouldn't end well for him. When he came home—*if* he came home—he'd likely lose pay and privileges. All those boys who defied the country's laws would.

"No, Finnie. I'll marry him the moment we see each other in London."

Her jaw dropped from the sheer lunacy of that rebelliousness. "How?"

"I can't worry about it now. I've got to get there first. The trip is long, two boat rides and a train from Liverpool to London. It'll take days, perhaps a week even, but—"

"Mary Violet Brennan!" Finnie's words were sharp with fear. "Have you lost your mind?"

"I've lost my heart," she answered with one of her musical laughs. "I canna go one more month without him or doing something about this wretched war. We're not neutral, Finnie. We're Ireland, and we're part of this world that is blowin' up. I have to help. I *have* to. I promised Timmy I would. I canna break my word."

Finnie searched her face, emotion welling up, along with a deep and abiding respect for Vi that was bigger than anything she'd ever known. Would she do the same if she were eighteen years of age? She liked to think she'd run from the farm to a boy she loved for a cause she believed in. She longed to have that kind of spirit, like her sister. But, still, this was lunacy.

"And how are you going to pay for this adventure, might I ask? You'll need to book passage."

For a long moment, Vi said nothing, and then she dug into her pocket and pulled out a kerchief rolled into a tight ball. Finnie instantly recognized the linen and lace she'd embroidered with Vi's initials two Christmases ago. "They have those carts that buy and sell goods near the port. I've seen them." She unraveled the lace and spread it. "I think one of them will buy something from me."

Finnie gasped at the treasures in her hands. Two glistening earbobs, a crystal paperweight she remembered from her granddaddy's workshop and… "Grandmammy's horseshoe pin? 'Tis unthinkable to sell!"

"'Tis *mine* to sell," she shot back. "All of this is. Given to me when she died, fair and square, to do with what I liked. I'm not stealin'."

"But that brooch is for your wedding. For good luck."

"Are ye not listenin' to me, lass? I'm marryin' Timothy Donovan!"

"But not with that brooch if it's sold to some cart vendor at Wexford Port."

Vi covered her treasures with the lace kerchief. "There's no wedding for me without Timothy, no matter how many of the local boys want to think differently."

Her voice cracked. "And there's no luck for the Irish if we don't do our holy duty and help win this war."

Finnie stared into the deep-blue eyes of a woman she loved and admired, a spark of passion flickering in her own chest. Vi was right. Timothy was right. Ireland shouldn't be neutral, couldn't be neutral in the face of the Nazis.

"I'll take you there." The words slipped out before Finnie had a chance to let good sense stop her. "I'll drive you to the port and bring the rig home after."

This time, it was Vi's eyes that widened, making her thick lashes brush close to the delicate arches of her brows. "Da would kill us both."

Except Vi would be gone, so Finnie alone would be on the receiving end of Da's wrath. But, what did a little strappin' matter? "'Tis the only way, Vi. We should leave now, before one of the boys is out here, cause not one of them will go along with this."

Reaching out, Vi's slender but strong fingers closed over Finnie's wool sleeve, pressing hard. "You can't drive to that place in the cart any more than you could fly to the moon. Tis much too far."

Finnie squared her shoulders. "If you can go to London, I can drive a cart to Wexford."

For a long moment, Vi's eyes coasted over Finnie's face, her eyes growing misty and warm. "You're a fine lass, Finola. A fine lass."

"And daft," Finnie whispered, giving her sister a gentle nudge. "Hurry now. We can get out the back path before Da knows we're even gone."

Chapter Five

Pru rolled over and opened one eye on Christmas Eve morning, happy to see the sun hadn't cracked the horizon yet. But it would soon, and once that happened, Waterford Farm would come to life. No matter the holiday, volunteers and staff would arrive to walk and feed the dogs, her uncles would show up for morning chores and the admin duties involved after a class of trainees left, and Grandpa would be heading into town for some kind of baked treats to warm up the kitchen.

But not yet, so Pru took a moment to close her eyes and remember Gramma's colorful, vivid story. As so often happened, the telling of the tale had exhausted the poor woman. Or at least, that's what she'd claimed when Pru begged to find out how the mysterious Vi Brennan kept the pin. Did she not go to war and marry Timothy Donovan, or did they get caught and strapped by the disciplinarian who was their father? Why had Gramma never mentioned her?

But Pru didn't have those answers. Before Gramma finished, she'd started to drift off, then patted the bed longingly, sending Pru off to her own room.

And Pru had gone to sleep thinking about that stickpin.

Despite its history, or maybe because of it, this pin was the exact something old that would make Mom's wedding day special. However, one shamrock was missing, leaving behind a sharp edge where it had been soldered on. In addition, the metal, certainly not gold, was rutted and tarnished, like it had been through the same war Violet and Timothy wanted to win.

Maybe they could fix or save the pin somehow and make it pretty enough that Mom could wear it on her dress or maybe on the lapel of her pretty cream jacket she'd be wearing from the church to the reception. But when and how? The jewelry-repair shop in Bitter Bark was closed today and wouldn't open until after the wedding.

But Aunt Darcy's fiancé, Josh, did construction and renovation, and he might have the tools they could use to fix the pin. Pru was certain she'd seen shamrock earrings in her grannie Annie's jewelry box once. Maybe Grandpa would let her have them, and Josh could somehow use them to mend the pin.

Liking this plan, Pru padded barefoot down the hall, happy to see Grandpa's door was still closed tight. Rusty was no longer sleeping outside of it, which meant Grandpa got home okay last night—but late. Rounding the bend to the third-floor stairs, she almost plowed into Gramma Finnie coming down.

"Oh!" They both drew back in surprise.

"I was just coming up to get you," Pru said. "I have an idea."

Gramma held out her hand, the pin in her palm. "I have a better one."

Pru laughed, mostly because Gramma Finnie had that spark in her eyes again. No matter what the idea was, it made her happy, so Pru was all in. "Tell me."

She leaned closer to whisper, "I did a little googlin' instead of saying my morning prayers," she admitted. "But one was answered anyway." Giving Pru the pin, she fished her phone out of her bathrobe pocket, tapping the screen with her index finger with the ease and comfort very few eighty-seven-year-olds had.

Pru fought another smile. She'd taught Gramma Finnie everything the old woman knew about technology, and it was a considerable amount.

"There's a place called Emerald Isle Jewelers that claims to be a 'Claddagh specialist,'" she whispered. "They repair vintage jewelry and specialize in mid-century pieces from Ireland."

"Really?" That was too good to be true. "Are they open?"

"Until three today, according to Google. And look here. 'We do repairs while you wait.'"

Pru scanned the screen and instantly found the address, and her heart dropped. Yep, too good to be true. "Who's going to take us to Holly Hills on Christmas Eve?"

"Me."

Pru choked. "I don't think so." Holly Hills was northwest, deeper into the Blue Ridge foothills and not the easy drive to Bitter Bark that Gramma Finnie could make in her Toyota Avalon.

"Child, hear me out. It's maybe two hours on a blue-sky day," she insisted. "I know the streets from long ago, so we can skip the big highway or interstate. I can handle it."

"I don't know, Gram—"

"I *need* to." She gripped Pru's arm. "I really need to."

Pru's heart tripped with love and the burning desire to make this woman happy. To see Gramma Finnie inspired and revitalized like she was that long-ago day in an Irish barn would be the best Christmas present to her whole family.

Or her mother might kill her for even considering it.

"I checked the weather already," Gramma added. "A dusting of snow to fall by afternoon, but we'll be home and making the Christmas Eve bread pudding by then. No one will even miss us."

"My mother and Trace will."

Gramma leaned closer. "She promised not to ask too many questions so you can surprise her. We can leave now, be there when the jeweler opens, and home by noon. We'll stay in touch by text, for sure, and trust me, child, your mother will have the best something old a Kilcannon lass could dream of wearing at her wedding."

"Did Vi wear it?" Pru asked.

Gramma's eyes closed for a moment. "You want to know? I'll tell you on the road."

"That's blackmail."

"Aye, 'tis." She grinned. "So, we can go on our little adventure?"

"Like Vi and Finnie?"

Gramma stared at her for a moment, then sighed, putting one hand on Pru's cheek. "Child, you are my heart and soul."

Pru patted the knotted knuckles, certain this small breaking of the rules was worth it. "Meet me at the kitchen door in ten minutes, and don't make a sound."

It took Gramma fifteen, but while she dressed, Pru wrote a note to Grandpa explaining that they'd be back by noon at the latest and not to worry. It was way too early to text Mom, so she would after seven. But if they dallied one more minute, Grandpa would come clomping down the stairs looking for coffee and insist on driving them. Then Gramma Finnie wouldn't have her adventure, and it would be like any other errand to run.

They hustled to the garage, where Gramma's pristine, rarely driven sedan was kept along with Dad's SUV. As they climbed in and Gramma slipped the key into the ignition, the two exchanged a gleeful look.

"I can't remember you looking this happy in a long time, Gramma Finnie."

She gave a slow smile. "May the road rise up to meet us and the wind be at our back."

"A fine Irish blessing for our trip." Pru held up her fist to bump knuckles. "Now, drive."

Gramma turned the key and looked over her shoulder…barely. "Is the garage door wide open?"

Oh boy. "Yes. Can't you see?"

"Just making sure." Her little shoulders squared, and she lifted up to look again. "Yes, there we go. It's open."

She hit the gas—a little hard—but backed out, and off they went with the rising sun and Waterford Farm firmly in the rearview mirror.

An hour and a half later, they were completely lost.

"I can't tell if the GPS isn't working out here, or if this road isn't even on any map, Gramma." Pru frantically tapped her phone, turning it around, looking up for a road sign, but they hadn't seen one since Gramma Finnie had insisted on taking a shortcut that bypassed the "traffic" in Bitter Bark. Which was maybe seven cars on Christmas Eve, when most of Bitter Bark was closed.

"No one knows about this route, not even those satellite leprechauns." Gramma Finnie leaned forward a little to squint at the road that was just this side of gravel instead of asphalt. "It used to belong to a Quaker family that moved here in the sixties. Anyway, it's a private pass and wouldn't be on that phone map."

She slowed to a stop at the intersection of a country road and a dirt path, looked left and right, and closed her eyes. "Left. I feel like it should be left."

"You *feel* like it?" Pru jabbed the phone screen again. "I feel like we need to listen to Google Maps."

Gramma reached over and patted her hand, pushing the phone onto Pru's lap. "What's the fun of that boring woman tellin' you where to go, child? I've lived here since 1954. I could walk to Holly Hills. Seamus and I used to go there every year for the Christmas festival. Nothing like Holly Hills at Christmastime."

"I know," Pru agreed. "I wanted to make a family outing this year again, but Mom was so busy with the wedding, I didn't even ask. That town sure takes its name seriously."

Holly Hills drew Christmas lovers the way Bitter Bark attracted families with dogs. From October to January, the Carolina mountain village was decorated to the nines for the holiday. "I love that Santa is on every corner, and all the elves walking around, and I read somewhere that they have three million lights or some crazy thing."

"Aye, and enough mistletoe to risk a rise in the birthrate nine months later." Gramma raised a brow and shot her a look. "And I speak from experience."

Pru giggled and settled into the seat, and the moment. "So you and Grandpa Seamus used to come here?"

"Oh yes. He loved to sing carols on the way over," she said. "Want to?"

"Sure. "Jingle Bells"? "All I Want for Christmas"? I guess "Grandma Got Run Over by a Reindeer" would be in poor taste."

She snorted. "What's poor taste is a carol without the true meaning of Christmas. I love the old hymns." She cleared her throat, sat up straighter, and barely skirted a pothole. "Hark! The herald angels sing…"

Pru cringed at the near miss, then joined in full force. "Glory to the newborn king."

"Peace on earth and…mercy!" Gramma slammed on the brakes so hard, Pru jerked forward. The seat belt smashed her collarbone and chest, trapping her gasp as she smacked her hands on the dashboard as the car came to a complete stop.

"What the—"

"Did you see it?" Gramma whipped around and looked at her, unfazed by the sudden stop.

"See what?"

"That dog!" She turned around and looked over her shoulder. "There's a dog on the side of the road."

Pru yanked at her seat belt, the need to take action zinging through her. "Is it hurt?"

"I don't know. But I don't want to back up in case it runs behind us."

"Where is it?"

"Back there, behind that big pine tree. Black and white."

Without waiting for more, Pru climbed out, leaving the car door open as she peered into the bushes, her heart rate kicking up as she searched.

"Hey, puppy," she called. "Anyone out here?" She glanced around the deserted rolling hills, not a house or car in sight. Had Gramma imagined the dog? Or had she seen something else? A deer? Bobcat? Good heavens, there were bears out here.

Maybe jumping out of the car hadn't been the *best* idea she'd ever had. Still, if it was a dog? It was the only idea. "Doggo? Come here, boy. Girl." She snapped her fingers, her gaze scanning for any movement. "Pooch?"

"I had treats in the glove box." Gramma Finnie came trotting around the back of the car with a spring in her step Pru couldn't remember seeing for months. Maybe longer. Her eyes glistened with enough inner joy to wipe away all of Pru's second thoughts.

Gramma waved a cookie in the air. "Treat!" she called. "What dog doesn't respond to that?"

Uh…a stray.

"Treat!" she yelled again.

Sure enough, there was a rustle in the bushes next to them. Pru turned, using her body to shield Gramma while she searched the foliage and waited, barely aware she held her breath.

They both jumped at the sharp, loud bark right before a two-toned face peered out from the bushes.

44

"Oh!" Pru exclaimed as Gramma went closer to the animal, holding out her treat.

"And what have we here?" she cooed. "Quite possibly the most beautiful thing these old eyes have ever seen."

"Speaking of eyes..." Pru inched closer, too, mesmerized by the set of eyes staring back at her. One was as blue as the skies over Waterford Farm on a midsummer day, the other a golden brown, both trained on Gramma and her treat. "Wow, that's a beautiful dog."

"Oh, she—or he—sure is." Gramma crouched over, still offering the cookie. "Are you a good one, too?"

They both knew dogs as well as people, and had this one been dangerous, it would have likely growled or bared its teeth by now. But Two Eyes just took a few more steps and relaxed its jaw into the closest thing to a smile.

Gramma set the treat on the ground, and the dog snatched it up in a second, then two arresting eyes looked up for more.

"Ah, yes, this is a fine border collie we've got here." Gramma reached out her hand, and the dog came closer, letting them see that she—Pru was guessing the gender but not sure—was bedraggled and dirty, with mud on her paws and dirt giving the white of her coat a grayish-brown tint. Her face was black with a white stripe down the front and a white snout, which somehow highlighted the mismatched eyes.

But she wasn't undernourished, that was for sure. On the contrary, that was one fat dog.

"Come here, darlin'," Gramma coaxed, getting another treat from her pocket. That's all it took to get the dog to give up all fear, head straight to Gramma Finnie to eat out of her hand...

And give Pru a clear view of a big belly, the cause of which didn't take a DVM degree to determine. "Definitely a girl," she said softly. "With a decent-sized litter on the way."

"In the family way, are ye?" Gramma slid her hands around the dog's face, then made a small squeal. "Thank the Lord, there's a collar and tag." She glanced at Pru. "I was scared she'd been abandoned."

"Let me see." Pru closed the space and crouched down, getting a whiff of filthy dog. "Not abandoned, but not exactly loved."

"Might have been lost for a while."

"Poor baby." Pru stroked her head, making sure the dog was completely comfortable with all this attention before attempting to read the collar tag. But the dog didn't take her eyes off Gramma Finnie, staring up as if she'd found her spirit animal, earth angel, and best friend all in the same creature.

And Gramma looked back at her with the same expression.

Pru angled the metal tag, but couldn't see anything on it. "Oh man," she muttered as she turned it over, hoping for a phone number or ID of some kind. There had been words imprinted, but they were impossible to read.

She tugged it closer and brushed away some knotted fur. "I can't read it. It's almost all worn off." Pru grunted in frustration as she searched for the collar latch under all the fur. "Let me look in the sunlight."

46

She snapped off the collar and turned to get full light on the cheap metal tag. Time and wear had faded the letters, but she could read some of them. A Q? The rest of the top word was completely missing. "Something that starts with B, then something something and an L, then something and a U, maybe an E."

"Blue." At the sound of Gramma sighing the word, Pru looked up to find her face-to-face with the dog, their noses practically touching. "It says Blue."

Technically, it didn't, but—

"What a beautiful name for you and that one blue eye, sweet lassie girl."

"I don't think the dog's name is—"

"Blue. It's perfect for her. She's Blue. My Blue."

Her...*wait a second.* "She's also super pregnant, lost, and filthy." Pru mustered her best General Pru voice, which she didn't have to use very often on Gramma Finnie. Her uncles sometimes, but rarely Gramma. But that was not Adventure Finnie, who seemed like a slightly different woman today. "We can't keep her, Gramma."

She straightened and turned to Pru. "But didn't we come to find something old, something new, something borrowed and..." Her brows lifted.

"Something blue," Pru finished.

"For a wedding with dogs, I can't imagine what could be better than a dog named Blue."

"Her name could be *Blunder* for all we know, and that's exactly what keeping her would be."

"Surely you canna leave her?" Gramma's brogue always grew thicker when something upset her.

"Of course not, but she has a collar, Gramma. That most likely means she has an owner. So, we'll take

47

her to the closest house and find out who owns her and return her. Then we'll go to Holly Hills and get that pin fixed, and then we'll go home." Because today's shenanigans didn't leave *that* much room for error.

"Child, you know abandoned dogs are a problem out here," Gramma Finnie said. "Garrett was just talking about it at Sunday dinner. People—if you can call them that—do leave dogs, especially pregnant ones."

"They wouldn't leave a dog with a collar that can be traced," Pru said, still trying to be the voice of reason.

"Garrett said it was why he calls this 'beagle season' for rescues. Those are hunting dogs that people pay to use for the season, then they don't want the expense of keeping them up." She shook head in disgust. "But we found you, Blue."

"We don't know she's been abandoned. She'd be spayed if she'd been a hunting dog. The males aren't neutered, but the females are. And border collies aren't hunting dogs. They don't have it in them to hurt a fly."

Gramma was too busy showering the dog with love to listen to reason, but that didn't stop Pru from trying.

"We need to try and find her owner."

Gramma tsked. "We don't have time to spend the day searching for an owner, lass."

Well, that much was true. But still, the idea of just walking off and keeping a collared dog was unthinkable. They had to at least try to find a local who knew the dog.

The dog nestled up next to Gramma, making a whimpering sound of true adoration.

"Aye, Blue. I love you, too."

Pru corralled all common sense since her great-grandmother had lost hers. "Look, let's do a search of the area by car for the nearest house and ask. If we can't find an owner, we'll bring her with us to Holly Hills and ask around. If we still don't have an owner, then we'll take her home and see if she's chipped, or Uncle Garrett can post her picture on one of his lost dog sites. If no one claims her, then..."

Gramma curled her hand into the dog's fur and turned toward the car like Pru wasn't even talking.

"Gramma Finnie."

"Hush, child." She flipped a hand over her shoulder, straightening to walk to the car. "We can do all that whatnot you suggested, but in the meantime, Blue and I will be good friends. Isn't that right, my love?"

Pru stood there and watched the old woman and the fat dog walk side by side. Blue waddled a bit with her distended belly, but Gramma still had that bounce in her step. Even more, now. And it was a wonder Blue could even walk straight, because she didn't take her heterochromatic eyes off her new pal.

Maybe she *was* abandoned, Pru thought. If that was the case, this pregnant pupper was coming home to Waterford Farm.

Chapter Six

There was a grand total of four houses spread out over the five-mile radius that Pru and Gramma Finnie managed to cover. At one, they met an older couple who were very nice, but had never seen the dog before. Another home had a young mother, alone with three kids, who was hesitant to even open the door. She peeked out and offered no clue who Blue belonged to, but suggested they try a new development about ten miles south where lots of people had dogs. No one was home at the other two places, one a small ranch with horses and a donkey, another just a simple, slightly run-down house that looked almost as abandoned as Blue.

Pru wrote notes, including her cell number, and left them stuck in both doors, then agreed they should head on to Holly Hills. But it was a wonder Gramma could even drive the remaining miles over rolling, rural hills surrounded by thick woods. She was distracted by the dog and lost all concentration, chattering on about all she knew about border collies, which was a surprising amount for a woman who'd owned setters her entire adult life.

"And you know what the Irish say about a dog with different-colored eyes, lass?"

"They see in color?" Pru guessed.

"Even better." Gramma sat up and threw a look in the rearview mirror. "'Tis said that when a dog has different-colored eyes, they go to heaven twice. Once while alive and again when they cross the bridge."

"You made that up," Pru said on a laugh.

"I did not!" On the vehement denial, she turned to check on Blue again, and the whole car veered dangerously out of its lane.

"Okay, okay, I believe you." Pru put a gentle hand on Gramma's arm. "Eyes on the road, please. I'll watch for a store where we can get Blue something to eat."

A few minutes later, they spotted a Dollar Tree and pulled in to get dog food and ask if they recognized Blue. No one did, but outside, the dog inhaled her lunch with gusto.

Finally, by some miracle and no accidents, they made it to Holly Hills in one piece, but much later than they'd planned. Main Street traffic was already clogged with tourists.

Only a little larger than Bitter Bark, Holly Hills was in full swing on Christmas Eve. Thousands of lights flickered, despite the fact that it was morning, and every sweet storefront tried to outdo its neighbor with over-the-top décor. Reindeer perched on rooftops, hosts of angels perched on streetlights, and Pru counted four men dressed as elves strolling the main drag. Every other shopper wore a Santa hat, all of them navigating around at least three different groups of carolers who meandered through the town square, providing music and entertainment.

"This is what Chloe imagined when she started the whole Better Bark program," Pru mused, remembering how her sister-in-law came up with the idea to change the name of their town for a year, turning it into the number one dog-friendly vacation destination in North Carolina, if not the world. "This is an insane amount of tourists."

"Well, 'tis Christmas Eve," Gramma said, gripping the steering wheel with white-knuckled hands as she steered clear of pedestrians and other cars. "And I think Chloe succeeded. Bitter Bark tourism is a crashing success, jam-packed with folk, both two- and four-legged. I think—oh!" She slammed on the brakes when a bike pulled out in front of her, and Blue slid forward on the back seat, giving out a soft yelp. "Is she okay?" Gramma turned, narrowly missing another pedestrian.

Pru fisted her own hands and realized she'd been holding her breath since...well, since Blue. She exhaled and rooted for calm in the face of Gramma Finnie's erratic driving.

"Okay, right after this stop sign, which you will obey by gently tapping the brakes, turn right into the visitors' parking lot. The jeweler is about two blocks, according to GPS. We'll walk the rest." *Or kill a tourist if we don't.*

"I think Blue can walk that," she said, following directions. "But only if she's comfortable and happy."

"She seems ready to go." Pru reached back and gave the dog a little head rub, which she took as an invitation to stick her head between the two front seats and rub her cheek on Gramma's jacket.

"Oh, my wee button of love!" Gramma patted her head...and drove right by the parking lot entrance.

They made it on the next pass, though, and soon they had Blue clipped on one of Meatball's leashes that Pru fortunately had had in her bag, then headed toward the center of town, to Emerald Isle Jewelers.

The small shop was open and already serving a few customers when they walked in and a blast of heat took the December chill off them.

"I'm sorry, service dogs only," one of the clerks called out, no doubt eyeing Blue's filth.

"Oh, darn." Pru took the leash from Gramma. "I'm so used to Bitter Bark, I forgot there are actual places you can't bring a dog. Should I stay outside with her or—"

Gramma's wide-eyed response answered the question. She was not leaving Blue.

"Then give me the pin, and I'll talk to them," Pru finished.

With a stern look at the clerk that said she did not like their policies or his judgy expression, Gramma opened her bag and pulled out the lace kerchief and handed it carefully to Pru. "Donchya be losing it or changing it, child. See if they have a shamrock to replace the missing one, and if not..." She looked down at it, and her lips pulled in a sad turn for the first time since they'd bumped into each other in the hall. "Then just have them clean it up and keep it as is. It doesn't have to be perfect."

For her mother's wedding? "Yes, it does."

"Then be careful with it."

Pru eyed the kerchief again, considering all the possibilities. "Are you sure you want to give it to them? It seems like it's dear to you."

She let out a sigh. "Ye have no idea, lass."

Something in Pru's heart twisted at the bittersweet lilt in her words. "Will you tell me?"

"Let's get it fixed for your mother first. Go on." She gave Pru a nudge. "The man's looking like he'll help you. I'll take Blue right out on that bench."

"Okay." Holding the pin, Pru headed to the counter, whispering a silent prayer that these people were really as Irish as the name of the business and would respect whatever history this piece had.

A few minutes later, she was certain they would. Not one but two clerks had already examined the piece, and the second went into the back to get the jeweler, who had the comforting name of Sean Hanrihan and specialized in Irish vintage jewelry.

Grateful for that good fortune, Pru spread the lace material on the glass counter, only then noticing the tiny MVB embroidered in the corner. A chill danced up her spine. Mary Violet Brennan, the great-aunt she hadn't known she had.

Why would she be wiped from family history? For going off to war?

Pru ran her finger over the tight, clean stitches, easily seeing that they bore Finola Kilcannon's signature style and realizing that this piece of linen and lace alone could be the something old if the jeweler didn't come through.

"Excuse me, miss?" An older man came out from the backroom, a bald grandfather type with a soft voice and kind eyes. "Are you the owner of this pin?"

"My great-grandmother, actually," she said. "Can you fix it?"

He had the pin on a piece of black velvet, which he set on the counter, making Pru wish Gramma had stayed with her, because he handled the pin with reverence, as if he knew the treasure's sentimental worth.

"I have some glass shamrocks at my studio at home that might fit the space, but it's going to take a few hours."

Her heart dropped in disappointment. "How many is a few?"

"We close at three today, so I could have it by then."

Three? She'd be toast with Mom if she didn't get home until late afternoon. But if they left at three, they'd be home in time for the Christmas Eve festivities, which would start around five or six. It could work. Mom would forgive her. "Okay, but if you could speed it up, I'd appreciate it."

He lifted the pin. "I don't want to rush this job. It's a rare style of jewelry you don't see much anymore."

"I know, and it's going on my mother's wedding dress as something old, so it has to be flawless."

He gave an understanding smile. "Flawless is the only kind of work I do."

She thanked him, filled out a form with contact information, and tenderly folded the hanky that had wrapped the pin for so many decades. Holding the delicate cloth to return it to Gramma, she stepped outside to break the news about the delay and call Mom, STAT.

But a huge group of carolers filed in front of her, filling the sidewalk with bodies and harmonies and bringing everyone else to a standstill. Pru leaned to one side, then the other, getting up on her tiptoes to look for Gramma and Blue on the bench just fifteen feet and forty singing Santas away, but she couldn't see a thing.

When they finally passed her, Pru stared at an empty bench. Then looked around. Up and down the street. Left. Right. Everywhere.

Holy St. Nicholas. Gramma was gone.

Chapter Seven

It probably would have been easier to check a weather app, but Molly was halfway between her vet office and the kennel before she even thought of that. If a snowstorm was coming, the dogs would know. And if the dogs knew, her brothers and her fiancé would know. Plus, family offered the added benefit of comfort, which was what Molly needed, along with the assurance that she might be overreacting to this minicrisis.

But the fact was, Pru hadn't answered a text in hours, and that just wasn't like her, no matter where she was or what she was doing.

As she reached the kennels, the door popped open, and the first face she saw was the man she loved most. Trace Bancroft's dark eyes inevitably softened when he looked at her or at their daughter. Since he'd returned to Bitter Bark almost a year ago to the day, the sight of this man's smile, the touch of his hand, and the whisper of his words of love in her ear had brought Molly unspeakable joy.

Her one-night stand at nineteen in the back of a minivan with Trace had miraculously turned first into

Prudence, the world's greatest child, and then a reunion romance that brought him back into her life. And next week they'd be married and official…except she couldn't think about that right this minute.

He reached out a callused hand to touch her face. "You haven't heard from Pru yet?"

He knew her so well, it was like she didn't even have to talk. She shook her head once, not trusting her voice.

"And she hasn't texted except that one time to say she and Gramma were running an errand and would be back soon?"

"At eight this morning," she said, checking her watch. "It's been hours, Trace. Gramma's not able to drive that far. What if they had an accident on the way to…" She grunted and dropped her head back in frustration. "I don't even know where she *is*. I took that app off my phone that tracks her, because it took up too much memory, and now I regret that."

"This is so not like Umproo," he mused.

She smiled at the nickname, a private joke born from Pru and Trace's first conversation, before either one knew they were father and daughter. "I would normally agree, but…" She shook her head.

"But what?"

"Oh, I overheard a conversation she had with Gramma Finnie yesterday, and I think they're both struggling a little right now. I want to give them time to work things out, but I can't help but worry that one's too old and the other's too young to be out and about without anyone knowing where they are. It scares me."

"What scares you?" Liam, her oldest brother, walked out of the kennel, a regal German shepherd gliding next to him. "This dog? Because he should, except watch this. Genghis. Sit."

The dog instantly sat.

"Greet."

He lifted a paw as if to shake Liam's hand.

"Cry for happiness."

Instantly, the dog flattened and let out a musical whine, making Molly laugh despite her heavy heart. "A killer, for sure."

"He will be when I'm done with him." Liam turned his full attention on her, searching her face with knowing eyes. "What's up, Molly? You don't look happy."

"I'm not." Behind Liam, she spied Garrett, her brother closest in age. As if he'd sensed an impromptu family meeting was happening, Shane showed up a second later.

"What's going on with you?" Garrett asked.

"Check her feet. They might be turning to ice this close to the big day," Shane teased as they formed a semicircle around her. The familiarity, love, and support of her brothers made Molly certain again that this response was the real reason she'd gone to the kennels when her low-grade anxiety about Pru grew to real worry.

"I am not getting—"

"Are we missing a family meeting?" Darcy called to the group as she and Josh approached, hand in hand. Their two little furballs, Stella and Kookie, broke off and ran toward the pen to play. "Because I do not like to miss family meetings."

As Darcy reached the group and she and her fiancé greeted the others, Molly and Trace exchanged a look.

He gave a slight nod of agreement to share what, at the moment, only they and her father knew. Dad was in town, but had been no happier about this turn of events when he'd left than Molly was.

"Gramma Finnie and Pru are…" *Missing.* No, that would send this crew into a rapid state of organized deployment of search parties and rescue teams. "Out."

The entire contingent of Kilcannons reacted with various forms of *yeah, and?* and *so what?* expressions.

"I don't know where they are," she added. Which did make them technically "missing," but not in the sense that it required action. Yet.

Still, they didn't look like they understood her concerns.

"Gramma's driving," Trace said, and that, of course, did the trick.

"Holy cow," Liam muttered. "That's not good."

"I knew we should have hidden her keys after she got pulled over for doing twenty-five in a fifty-five zone," Darcy mused.

"Don't worry, I've caught Pru driving that Jeep a dozen times." Garrett gave Molly's shoulder a reassuring pat. "She can drive if push comes to shove."

"Push could come to shove," Shane said, shaking his head. "Last time she drove in the rain, I had to push that Toyota out of the mud when she went left when the driveway veered right. The *driveway*," he repeated. "Forget the highway."

Molly glared at him. "You're not helping."

"Just saying you're not crazy for worrying, Moll."

She glanced at Trace. "Where could they go and be gone for hours? They left before Dad even got up."

"He's in town," Darcy said. "Did you tell him to look around for Gramma's Avalon? They might just be shopping, and if they hit Bitter Bark Yarn and Fabric? Gramma could be lost in there for hours."

Molly appreciated the logic and reassurance, but the silent phone in her hand told a different story. "Dad's looking for them, but I think they're on a special errand, and it may have taken them out of Bitter Bark."

"What kind of errand?" Garrett asked.

"Something for the wedding," she said. "I gave them what I thought was a simple job, because both of them were unhappy. Pru was feeling left out of the wedding plans, and Gramma was feeling..." She hadn't heard what was bothering Gramma, but had had a few conversations with her lately that had led Molly to think she might know. "Old and unimportant."

"Unimportant?"

"Are you kidding?"

"This place would go up in flames without her."

"And no bread pudding?" Josh looked horrified. "'Cause *that's* important."

Their laughter made Molly feel a little better. "I'm probably overreacting," she said. "But I am concerned about the weather."

"Me too," Liam said, absently scratching the head of his current trainee. "The dogs that react to a pressure drop, which is most of them, are definitely on edge."

"We're getting some snow," Garrett confirmed. "We got a call to pick up a rescue in Boone, and I couldn't even promise I could make it today. They're going to get socked in up there."

She glanced toward the Blue Ridge Mountains at their horizon. Would Gramma Finnie and Pru drive west for anything? Of course not. They wouldn't go farther than the next town over. Would they?

"Chill, baby." Darcy slipped her arm around her big sister. "Pru's more responsible than all of us combined, and Gramma's not going to go far. I'm sure they got caught up doing something fun and forgot the time. And we can all keep calling and texting her, so they know to hightail it back home ASAP."

Molly gave her a squeeze and let them all know with hugs and smiles how much she appreciated this family.

"Don't worry, babe," Trace said, pulling her into him. "You can't change a thing by worrying. You want to take a drive and start looking?"

She turned over her phone and stared at the text messages again. Delivered. Not read. Why wouldn't Pru read her messages? What could she be doing? What if she was hurt? Or maybe they were in a dead zone for phone service? But this long? Did that mean they were stuck somewhere, or had an accident?

She swallowed hard and nodded. "Yes, I do. Let's head toward Chestnut Creek to see if we can spot them."

"Take the Jeep." Garrett tossed his keys to Trace. "In case you run into weather."

"We better not," Molly murmured.

"Just keep us posted on the family group text," Liam added.

"And I'll poke around Gramma's room for clues," Darcy said.

"I'll call the fire station and see which of our cousins is on duty today." Garrett pulled out his phone. "They can put the sheriff on notice to look for Gramma's car."

She looked from one sibling to another, awash in gratitude. "I didn't want this to turn into a Kilcannon code red, you guys."

"Just pink," Shane said with a wink. "We're on call for when you need us."

Thanking them, Molly slipped her hand into Trace's and headed off to the Jeep. She could count the times Pru had given her cause to worry. But deep in her gut, she sensed that this time, something was really wrong.

"Gramma! Gramma Finnie!" Pru clutched the kerchief and spun around to scan the busy street. Shoppers, pedestrians, and, good heavens, *more* carolers blocked her view and made her wish that last few inches of height Mom kept promising had actually happened in her last growth spurt. But at five feet, three inches, Pru couldn't see over much taller heads and shoulders.

She made her way through the crowd to the street, which was bumper to bumper with stalled holiday traffic. Where would she go?

"Excuse me," she said to a couple settling on the bench where Gramma was supposed to be. "Did you see an older woman here? With a black and white dog?"

The woman frowned and shook her head.

"It was a really distinct-looking collie with two different-colored eyes."

"Oh." The man sat up and gestured down the street. "I did notice that dog. I saw it right at that crosswalk, headed to the other side of the street."

Why would she leave? "Thank you!" Pru barely got the words out before taking off toward the intersection, coming to a screeching halt at the Don't Walk sign. Instantly, she could practically feel the torment rip her body in half.

Pru would sooner cross the street naked than disobey the sign. Like the other pedestrians, she waited, bouncing on her sneakers, itching to break this rule. Across the street, the crowd was even denser where diners waited outside of two crowded restaurants and a line formed to sit on Santa's lap in a bookstore.

But there was no sign of an old lady and a dog. *Where are they?*

While she waited, she whipped out her phone and let her thumbs fly in a quick text to Gramma. *WHERE ARE YOU?*

She didn't wait for an answer as panic rose, and the light stayed red. She looked left and right, but the traffic was at a dead stop anyway. With a single breath for courage, she put her foot on the street, held up a hand to the cars, and somehow crossed Main Street, feeling no less victorious than Moses making it to the other side of the Red Sea.

"Gramma!" she called again, her voice tight with a pounding pulse.

The entire family would never forgive her if something happened to Gramma Finnie. Pru's life would be over. She'd be an outcast, sent away to live as a pariah, and Mom would probably not get married out of grief. Pru would never recover from the guilt.

The car! Maybe Gramma went to the car to get something for Blue. Turning, she ran toward the lot, peering at the face of every person under five feet. No Gramma. No dog. No nothing. Why didn't she—

Pru felt her phone vibrate in her pocket and almost tripped on a cobblestone when she slammed to a stop to fish it out. On a noisy exhale, she whipped out the phone, scooted out of the flow of traffic, and looked at the words that appeared on her screen before she even opened the text.

Pru, I am not happy that I haven't heard from you for so many hours. You know better than to do this. Where are you? When are you coming home and wh...

"Oh." She didn't even tap the screen to read the rest of Mom's rant. It would just make her feel worse. What could she say? *I'm fine, but Gramma disappeared.*

Think, Prudence Anne. Think straight.

First, the car. She retraced the route to the parking lot, jogged past the booth at the entrance, and tore to the Toyota Avalon parked along a wall.

Coming around the back, her heart dropped when she didn't see anyone inside. No Gramma, no dog. With a grunt, she smashed her face to the driver's window, cupped her hands, prayed for a miracle, and saw...Gramma's phone on the console.

She almost howled in frustration.

Without taking one more minute, she shook off the panic and headed back to where the guy had said he'd noticed Blue. Back through the crowds and carolers, sweat dripping underneath her down coat and thick sweater, the Christmas-colored world blurring around her as tears filled her eyes.

Finally, she stopped to catch her breath, leaning against the glass of a storefront, coming to terms with the fact that she had two choices: call the police or run away from home. Then she felt the glass behind her shake a little, like someone was knocking on it. Probably the owner telling her to stop blocking their display.

Another knock. Louder.

She whipped around to wave an apology, coming face-to-face with a dog. And not any dog. The sudsy head of a dog with two totally different colored eyes staring back at her.

"Blue!"

She jerked back to get some perspective, realizing she was standing in front of a pet store that put their groomers in the window and—

"You found us." Gramma Finnie came out of the door, looking calm, cool, and completely fine.

Pru almost screamed with a full-body jolt of relief and anger. "Where have you been?"

"I was headed back to you, lassie," she said, waving a dismissive hand as if going MIA in a strange city was perfectly normal. "But Blue, oh, she does attract attention. So while you were in the jewel shop, I met a really nice lady who works here as a groomer. Well, she's a vacation fill-in, actually, but she just moments ago had an unexpected cancellation, and that's why she was getting lunch, so..." Her gaze shifted to the window behind Pru. "Look at my sweet Blue."

Pru's heart almost returned to normal. Almost. "Gramma, you can't just leave me in a strange town and not tell me where you're going. And without your phone!"

Her old eyes shuttered closed. "I'm not a wee five-year-old, nor have I lost my faculties, and have you never forgotten your phone in your life? I'm one block away from that bench."

"But this place is crazy busy," she said. "Anything could have happened to you."

"Aye." She gave that bittersweet smile. "Told you I had a bit of a reckless streak when I was younger. But, then, I'm not young anymore."

Irritation mixed with regret, because Pru had made her feel old and, well, not reckless. "I realize you want to have fun and spread your wings and not be bored, but that doesn't mean you can leave me in a state of panic. Not to mention…" She looked at her phone, and there was yet another text from Mom. All caps this time. "I'm doing the same thing to my mother. I have to call her." She glanced from side to side, looking for a quiet place to do that, but nothing in Holly Hills on Christmas Eve was quiet.

Gramma's wrinkled old face softened. "Aye, lass, you're right. I'm sorry for putting you in a state. It's over now, and we just have to wait for Blue, then we can head right back home."

"Except we have to wait until later this afternoon for the pin," Pru said, handing her the empty kerchief. "That's the bad news. The good news is the jeweler thinks he has a shamrock that will work."

"Oh, sure 'tis good news. And I'm hungry, so let's find some lunch and make up from our harsh words and find a place to call your mother and…" Her gaze dropped to the lace-trimmed hankie she was threading through her fingers, pausing as she rubbed the stitching of MVB.

"Did you do that?" Pru asked. "Did you embroider your sister's handkerchief?"

She didn't answer for a long time, staring at the cloth. "I did, but when you think…" She closed her eyes and lifted the hankie to her nose, taking a deep breath. "It's like I can still smell the waterfront that day and hear the shouts of the street vendors, the clang of the sales, and the buzz of excitement and danger in the air."

"No, that's Holly Hills on Christmas Eve." Pru put her hand on Gramma's shoulder. "And I see a deli up there that might not have a wait for lunch if you're willing to sit at the counter. Come on. I'll call Mom and tell her where we are, but not what we're doing, and you can tell me what happened the day you took your sister to the port."

Gramma smiled. "Oh, child. What happened that day was nothing short of a Christmas miracle." She sniffed again. "And I *can* smell the air that day. And I can remember it, plain as day. I'll never, ever forget the way he looked at me."

"He?" The word caught Pru's attention as they walked. "Your dad? The man who ran the cart? Timothy, the soldier Vi wanted to marry? Who is he?"

Gramma just smiled and slipped her hand through Pru's arm. "Oh, I'll tell you, lass. I'll tell you all about him."

Chapter Eight

Wexford Harbor, Ireland

Wet snow and rain pressed scratchy wool to Finnie's shivering body. Her arms ached from clinging to the rough rope of Alphonsus's harness. Her backside felt as broken as the road they'd traveled to get here. And she was so hungry it felt like her empty belly was turning inside out in search of a morsel.

But as they climbed out of the cart and took in the wild, loud, frightening vista of Wexford's port, Finnie caught a glimpse of her sister, and all of her discomfort disappeared.

Vi practically glowed. Yes, she was as soggy as Finnie and surely as cold and hungry after a ride over the most rutted, impossible trail from just outside Carrig Hill to the largest harbor in the county. But here she was, at the end of a journey of several hours, and Vi's eyes were bright, her cheeks rosy, and her smile firmly in place.

"Let's find the cart vendors," she said, squaring her

shoulders after they hitched Alphonsus to a post sticking out of a stone wall for just that purpose. "They're like money changers."

They were more like thieves to hear Da tell about it. But for many people, there was no other way to get passage on a boat. The tickets were costly, and poor country folk had little cash on hand if they needed to make an emergency trip. So someone was always available to take what they had to sell—even family treasures.

Finnie followed, swallowing her sadness about a piece of jewelry. All the way to the port, Vi had nattered on about the war, the dead, the troubles in England. They simply had to beat the Germans, and Ireland's neutrality was a national embarrassment.

Lots of Irish felt that way, Finnie knew. Not the mothers, of course, but the young men. Plenty of lads wanted to fight.

In fact, some were right here. Two here, another group of four or more over there, all fit and hearty and barely twenty. Heck, some were not quite seventeen. And every cluster they passed, Finnie felt their gazes move to Violet.

Her sister didn't notice as she wove her way to a row of cart vendors, some selling, some buying, a little livestock on one, some flowers and vegetables on another. But at the end, one could find the "goods," as they were called. The keepsakes. The family heirlooms and precious gemstones. The dear things that made a house a home. All sold for very little so someone could go somewhere.

So sweet country nurses could go to London and save lives and get married.

"This one," Vi said, holding Finnie's hand to keep her close and bring her along. "I like this one."

Finnie squinted at the cart display of ribbons, hats, and a velvet box of some inexpensive jewelry. Behind that stood a man with steely eyes beneath a paddy cap pulled low. He huddled into a herringbone wool jacket, a cigarette dangling from his fingers.

As they got closer, Finnie held back. "I don't like this one," she muttered.

"Come on. He has earbobs. He'll like mine." She approached the cart and got his attention immediately.

"Sellin' or buyin', lassies?" The man sounded nicer than he looked, but Finnie still lingered a bit away while Vi approached the cart. She couldn't hear what they were saying, thanks to the clanging of metal and the shouts from men working on the docks. A horse and buggy rattled by, and two men argued furiously over the price of something.

Finnie tucked herself deeper into her coat, closer to the next cart than the one where Vi was negotiating away family treasures.

"It's all I got, sir, but 'tis a fine lamp."

Finnie turned at the sound of a young man's voice—no, not quite a man yet, she realized as her gaze landed on a customer at the cart behind her.

"Aye, lad, I feel the ache in yer gut," the cart vendor said, spitting to the side to punctuate the sentence. "But I canna gi' you a dime for that."

Finnie inched closer, drawn for some reason to the youthful face. Did he want to go to the war, too? He was far too young to fight, Finnie thought, taking in baby-soft skin and clear eyes that shifted between green and brown. His hair was long and tousled, and his narrow shoulders rose and fell with a huge sigh of disappointment.

"I need the money, sir," he pleaded. "I have to go."

The cart vendor shook his head vehemently. "Donchya go, lad. You'll be dyin' like all the rest of them. There's a reason Ireland's neutral."

So he was going to war. Or trying to.

"I have to go," he insisted. "My brother went. He's there, waitin' for me."

Like Timothy Donovan. Everyone there was waiting for someone.

The cart vendor pulled his flat cap lower and leaned into the lad's face. "And what about when you get home? *If* you get home. Won't be a hero, that's for sure."

"I don't care about being a hero," he said defiantly. "You want them to win? They're bombing London. They'll take Ireland! They won't stop!"

"You're not going to stop the Germans, lad."

"I could try!" he insisted. "I have to go. 'Tis what I am meant to do."

"We're Ireland, not Europe, lad. Now take your little lamp home to yer mammy and get off the docks."

Color rose in his cheeks, accenting a peppering of freckles on his smooth skin and turning his eyes coppery and cold. "We can't lose this war, man."

"*We* are not in a war, lad." He turned away to another customer, leaving the young man standing stone-still. After a moment, he looked up, directly at Finnie.

He stared at her like he could see right through her, like he could peer into the depths of her soul, and he let her have a glimpse of his. What she saw was pure…goodness. So honest and real that she could feel her next breath strangle in her chest. She wanted to—

"Let's go, Finnie! Let's go." Vi grabbed her arm and jerked her around, yanking her closer. "I saved the pin!" She let out one of her tinkling laughs. "I saved it for you."

"And still got enough money?"

Her sister shoved the kerchief into Finnie's hand, and the pin poked her palm like a little reminder that they still had that one treasure. A stick in the hand had never felt so good.

"More than enough. Granddad's paperweight paid for the fare to Dublin, and the earbobs will get me all the way to London."

"Then you take it." She offered the tiny bundle back to Vi. "For your wedding day."

But Vi shook her head defiantly. "'Tis my gift to you, sweet sister. To thank you for bringing me here today, even though you'll pay a price." She pressed her hands to her mouth, practically dancing on her toes with excitement. "This is it, sweet Finnie. I'm going to Timmy. Going to save lives. 'Tis what I am meant to do."

'Tis what I am meant to do.

The echo of the lad's words made Finnie turn back to where he still stood, listening to their exchange. She saw the moment Vi's words hit his heart, and jealousy and heartache crashed over him. She felt his pain in the pit of her stomach.

"Let's go," Vi insisted. "I need to get my bag from the cart, and heavens above, lass. You have to get home, or there's no tellin' what Da will do."

She dragged Finnie back to the stone wall and hitching post, chattering the whole way like she'd just bought passage to the countryside for a holiday, not to London in the middle of a bombing.

At their cart, Vi reached into it and pulled out a small cloth bag and the leather case with the nurse's cross that Mammy had given her for her birthday. She hoisted it high like a trophy.

"I'm off to nurse, lassie."

The realization of what she was doing and where she was going slammed Finnie as though Alphonsus had lifted his front leg and clomped her in the chest. "Mary Violet, please be careful. And write. And come home."

She tipped her pretty head and added a smile that no doubt kept Timothy Donovan alive just thinking about it. "Aye, my dear sister. I will. In that order." She held out the bags for a hug. "C'mere, wee one. Ya know I've always loved you best of all the whole Brennan clan. You be kind to our brothers, now."

"Patrick wants to go, too, you know." She'd heard her sixteen-year-old brother talk about it far too often.

"Then maybe I'll see him there."

Saints alive, *two* Brennan kin at war? "I canna think about that," Finnie admitted.

"Listen to me." Vi took Finnie's face in two gloved hands. "Donchya be afraid of anything, lass. If you need to do something, do it. If yer heart feels a callin', listen to it. Be a wee bit more reckless, my sweet Finola, like you were today. It will free your soul." She finished her speech with a kiss on Finnie's cheek.

Fighting a sob, Finnie wrapped her arms around

her sister, inhaling her flowery, familiar scent, then stood like a statue to watch Vi practically skip toward the docks, swinging her nurse's bag. Finally, when the last bit of auburn hair disappeared, Finnie turned to pat Alphonsus on the head and climb into the cart.

Just as she got settled on the bench, she saw him again. The lad with the green-gold eyes and good heart. He was walking toward her, his body shoved deep into a navy coat, hands stuffed into the pockets, head down against the sleet that had just started to spit from the clouds.

"Do you want a ride?" Her question tumbled out before Finnie could stop the words. *There you go, Vi. A wee bit reckless.*

He looked up, slowed his step, and a shadow of a smile crossed his face. "To Dublin, aye. And then to England."

She nodded. "My sister just left. She's a nurse."

His eyes flashed with envy. "Lucky."

"Not sure I'd call her that," Finnie said. "I'm going to Carrig Hill if you—"

"She's lucky," he insisted. "But I'm a man, and I'm the one who should go to war."

"A man?" Finnie couldn't keep the doubt out of her voice. "Don't look much older than I am, which is barely twelve and a half."

"I'm fifteen," he said, turning to steal a look at the docks. "Old enough to fight for what matters. To fight for the world." He leaned closer, and once again, Finnie had that feeling like the very world was a little off-kilter. Was that how Vi felt when she looked at Timmy? Because it was…nice.

"Sorry you can't go," she said.

"Not as sorry as I am," he replied. "I left my family, who might not even want me back. I left a good job as an apprentice glassblower. I left everything because of what I believe in, but no one wants this." He pulled a wicker flame lamp out of his pocket and turned it over. "And now my mam'll kill me for taking it, but it was all I could think of to get passage."

It didn't look like much of a treasure, so 'twas no wonder he couldn't sell it. Not like…not like…

She looked down at her hands and the wrinkled kerchief wrapped around a real treasure.

"And thank you for the offer, miss, but I'm heading back to County Waterford."

Waterford? "That's so far."

"I'll make it." He added a half smile, and that just made her heart turn in her chest. "But 'tisn't where I want to go. Not by a long shot."

He *could* go. He could realize his dream. And what would it cost her?

If you need to do something, do it.

She'd thought she was parting with the pin today anyway, and this lad, this sweet, handsome lad full of heart and passion…she could help him. It could be Finnie's own little sacrifice to save the world.

If yer heart feels a callin', listen to it.

She leaned forward and held out her linen-and-lace-wrapped package. "Here."

He drew back, frowning, looking from her hand to her face.

"Take it," she insisted. "'Twill buy your passage."

His jaw loosened as he lifted his hand to take what she offered.

"Should get you to Liverpool," she said, remembering what Vi had told her. "After that, you might have to get creative."

Slowly, he unwrapped the kerchief with as much care as he might give a valuable Christmas present. As he saw the pin, his eyes widened. After a moment, he looked up at her, silent, but she could read his expression. *Gratitude.*

"You take it," she said. "On one condition."

"You want my lamp?"

She laughed. "You come back."

He blinked at her. "Aye, lassie. I'll come back. I swear on it. And thank you, Miss…Miss…"

"Brennan. My name's Finola Brennan."

"Finola Brennan." It sounded like a song on his lips, then he pressed the kerchief and pin to his chest. "I thank you, Finola." He nodded a few times, backing away as if he thought she might change her mind. "Thank you," he muttered again, turning to run toward the carts.

"Wait!" she called.

He hesitated, but didn't stop at first, no doubt worried she'd ask for the pin back. But then he finally halted and turned. "Aye?"

"What's your name?" she asked. "So I can pray for you." *And think about you every night.*

"My name's Seamus," he said, adding a grin of relief that she hadn't changed her mind. "Seamus Kilcannon."

She nodded, taking the name into her heart and finding a place where she could keep that name safe and sound. "You be careful, Seamus Kilcannon. And remember your promise."

He just smiled and lifted the pin, the white lace kerchief fluttering in the wind. "I'll be back, Finola Brennan. And when I do, when this war is over, I won't forget this act of kindness. I'll kiss ye for it. I promise that, too."

Chapter Nine

Pru gasped so hard she almost choked. "That's how you met Great-Grandpa Seamus? You were *twelve*? And gave him that pin? And, wait, how did you get it back, and did he get hurt, and what about your sis—"

"Lass." Gramma put a weathered hand on Pru's arm. "Your phone is ringin'."

Oh God. *Mom.* "I forgot to call her! I got so involved in that story." Pru scrambled to snag her phone, pulling her head into the present after Gramma's journey to the past, shared while they waited for lunch at the deli counter.

She frantically tapped the screen before the call went into voice mail and pressed her cell phone to her ear. "Mom, Mom. I'm here."

"Pru!" Three letters, one syllable, so much shock, guilt, anger, and dismay.

"I'm fine, Mom. We're fine."

"Where *are* you?"

Pru exhaled. "Holly Hills. We had to—"

"Gramma Finnie drove to Holly Hills?" Mom

wasn't usually a shrieker, but this time her voice was so loud, Gramma drew back and made a face.

"She did great," Pru said. "And I told you we had to run an errand. A *wedding* errand." That should get her out of a little trouble, right?

"So you let an eighty-seven-year-old woman drive into the mountains in the dead of winter?"

"There was no weather. And no problems." Well…if you didn't count picking up a stray and nearly losing Gramma completely. "We'll be home later this afternoon, I swear."

"Pru, there's snow coming. Please come home now. No wedding errand is worth your safety."

She couldn't get that pin back now, could she? That jeweler said he was taking it home. "I'll try."

"No try. *Do.*"

Pru attempted a laugh. "Sure thing, Yoda."

"Pru, I am not happy with you right now." Mom was working to keep it together, she could tell. Guilt nearly strangled Pru when she thought about the wedding stress, the holidays, and Mom was probably missing her own mother right now. As great an idea as this had seemed in the moment, it suddenly felt kinda dumb.

"We'll leave right away…if we can."

"What do you mean 'if we can'?"

She exhaled slowly. "We found a dog and—"

"A dog?"

"Abandoned in the hills, and so we're just waiting to get her cleaned up and…"

"Is she sick?" she asked, always a vet to the heart.

"If you consider pregnancy an illness," Pru said, biting her lip.

"You found a pregnant dog?" It was clear from the sound of her voice that Mom didn't know whether to laugh or cry over that one.

And she really didn't want to give up on that pin. "Oh, Mom, this dog is so cute. Gramma's in love. She's a border, with one blue and one brown eye, which are so—"

"Bring the dog home now, and you'll beat the snow. Please, Pru."

She squeezed her eyes shut. "But, Mom, we're waiting for one more thing, and it's really important, and you *have* to—"

"Umproo." Trace Bancroft's low voice cut off her plea, and she could picture him taking the phone, flexing his tattooed biceps, and sliding into Dad mode, which came more and more naturally to him every day. "You need to listen to your mother. To both of us. Come. Home. Now."

She swallowed and slid a look to Gramma as their sandwiches were placed in front of them. "Okay, we just got lunch, so—"

"*Now.*"

She nodded in silent resignation. "All right, Trace. Tell Mom we'll be home soon." She set the phone down and stared at Gramma. "We are currently in some exceedingly deep doo."

Gramma smiled. "Kind of like what happened to me that day when I got home from Wexford Port."

Pru looked longingly across the table. She needed to hear the rest of that story. But they had to move. *Now.*

"Let's get the sandwiches to go, Gramma, and spring Blue from the groomers. I'll run into the jewelry store and tell them I can't pick up the pin until…" She shook her head. "Maybe Trace or one of my uncles will drive me back here after Christmas."

Gramma Finnie just sighed in agreement, accepting their fate and her role in it.

A few minutes later, they walked into the groomer's studio, only to be met by the owner, a platinum blonde wearing a paw-print patterned apron with the name Melanie embroidered on the chest.

"You've found Queenie!" The woman rounded the counter with her hands outstretched to greet them. "She's been missing for almost two weeks. Jenny didn't know her, of course, but I recognized her the minute I came back from lunch."

"So you know her owner?" Pru asked.

"Oh yeah. Old Bill Cutter even came in here with a sign for our lost-dog board out front. Didn't you see it in the window? And, believe me, it takes a lot to get that old fart out of the house." She snorted. "But he'd do anything for Queenie."

"Queenie?" Gramma Finnie repeated the name like it was the dumbest thing she'd ever heard.

"Bill Cutter." Pru pictured the owner's name in her head, seeing the B, l, u, and e and all those missing letters. "That's what's on her tag." And a name that began with a Q. Now it all made sense. "So she has an owner."

"Oh, she has an owner all right, and if he thinks you've been messing with his girl, he'll let you know about it with one of his shotguns." The woman hooted and shook back thick waves of hair. "Just kidding. Kinda."

"We'll have to return her on our way back to Bitter

Bark," Pru said, putting a light hand on Gramma's shoulder because she sensed this news wasn't going to make her happy.

"Bitter Bark?" Melanie's brows shot up. "Wrong direction, hon. He lives in the mountains a good ten miles west and north of here. Maybe fifteen. You won't find his place on GPS, and I don't even have an address, but I can draw a map."

Draw a map? What was this? The 1400s? "How about we just call him?" Pru suggested.

"If he had a phone, which he does not."

"Then let's forget about it," Gramma said. "He doesn't love Blue enough to take care of her—"

"Gramma." Pru narrowed her eyes. "We can't *steal* the dog."

Melanie snorted. "You can try, but I guarantee you old Bill would hunt you down and get her back and make you pay for his inconvenience. That old piece of crust hates everyone and everything except that dog."

"Didn't love her enough to get her spayed," Gramma noted. "It's the right thing to do for a dog."

Melanie nodded in agreement. "But he lives like a hermit in the woods. He didn't think it was necessary, which, of course, I didn't agree with. And one time she got out, and sure enough, some hunting dog had his way with her."

"Now he'll have a litter to take care of," Gramma said. "Probably more than he can handle."

"Who knows?" Melanie shrugged. "Might get him out more often. I'm telling you, the man's got agor…agor…he hates to leave the house."

"Agoraphobia?" Pru suggested.

"Yeah, that. Except for Queenie," she replied. "He comes in here for supplies ever since he got Queenie a few years back. Now? I don't know what's going on, because he thinks she's dead."

"Oh." Pru pressed her hand to her chest. "He needs his dog back."

"That he does," Melanie said. "I saw him cry when he brought that picture, which really shocked me. He's a Vietnam vet, a Marine sniper with more than fifty confirmed kills, they say."

With each piece of Bill Cutter's puzzle, Pru got a little more upset. "Sure don't want to get on the wrong end of *that* rifle. We have to return her, Gramma. Or could you board her here?" The idea popped into Pru's head and suddenly made so much sense.

But Melanie gave a negative shake of her head. "Sorry. We're beyond overbooked for Christmas. And..." She checked her watch. "We're closing in a few minutes for the Elf Parade. But I can get you to his woods, then he'll find you, believe me."

He'd find them? *In the woods?* "I can't take the—"

"I'd take her myself, but I'm on the Elf Parade judging committee. But I'll tell you this, he's a broken man. You get that dog to him today, and you'll give Bill Cutter the best Christmas present he's ever had."

When Melanie finally paused for a breath, Pru turned to look at Gramma. "There's really no discussion," she said.

"Aye. Not even your mother could say no. 'Tis the right thing to do."

"Uncle Liam would be furious if we didn't help out a fellow Marine."

Gramma put a hand on Blue's head. "As long as she is well loved."

"I'll text Mom," Pru said, taking out her phone before she forgot again, tapping furiously.

Found dog's owner! We're returning her (of course!) and then will be on our way home. Love ya!!

She added a few pink hearts for good measure, still thinking through the timing.

"You know, Gramma, on the way back, we'll come through town and get the pin. I'll stay in constant contact with my mother, so we can't—"

"Blue!" Gramma called out the name as their groomer came through the door with the dog trotting next to her, wearing a sparkly blue and white bandanna, her fur all clean, trimmed, and lovely.

"I thought you said her name was Blue," the young groomer said. "That's why the bandanna. But Mel told me it's Queenie."

"It's Blue today." Gramma crouched down to greet the dog, who headed right to her, tongue out. Without a command, she dropped in front of Gramma Finnie, looking up with her haunting mismatched eyes locked on her new favorite person.

"There's my sweet lassie."

"Oh, she likes you." The owner came closer.

"Of course she does." Gramma leaned closer and rubbed the dog's head with both hands. "I found her pregnant, alone, scared, and starving."

"True, but she's generally a one-man dog. Course, those pregnancy hormones are raging." She grinned. "They sure can change a personality."

"Her personality is perfect." Gramma Finnie scratched her head some more. "And I love her."

Pru stepped closer and put her arm around her great-grandmother. "Then you should love her enough to get her home for Christmas."

"Aye," she said. "I know that, child."

"And it sounds like meeting Bill Cutter will be another adventure," Pru added.

That made Gramma smile, and Pru had to remember that that was the real purpose of this trip.

Chapter Ten

Pru's sense of satisfaction disappeared the minute they walked outside to find the first fat snowflakes falling. The tourists of Holly Hills cheered, and the two groups of carolers started dueling with *White Christmas* and *Winter Wonderland*, while the retailers flashed their lights with holiday happiness.

They were Christmas crazy, and Pru was about to be grounded for life. "You can't drive in the snow," she exclaimed to Gramma.

Gramma turned her face toward the sky and kept it there while two snowflakes hit her glasses. Another landed on her cheek. "Hush, child. 'Tis barely a drop."

Now. But how long until it started to build up on the road and make it slippery and dangerous as they headed into the mountains?

Pru zipped through her options. They couldn't just go home with this dog, could they? No. It didn't feel right in her heart. A man who suffered from a debilitating disease had lost his best friend and possibly his reason for living. On Christmas Eve! They had to go.

"We'll be there and back before an inch falls," Gramma assured her, as if she'd read her mind. "And if it gets thicker, we'll call Waterford for help." She added a sly smile. "We're already in loads of trouble, child. How bad can it be?"

Pru stifled a moan. "Bad."

But Gramma and Blue powered on back to the parking lot, the two of them weaving their way around pedestrians and lampposts, side by side. Blue stopped once, and they thought she might find a little grass to pee on, but she just sat on the curb and panted a bit, and, of course, Gramma Finnie waited patiently. It took a precious fifteen minutes to persuade her to get up and back to the car.

"It's all so unusual for her, I suppose," Gramma said as they drove off and away from the hustle of Main Street. "Poor dear."

Pru spread the map the lady had made them and took her first real good look at it, which only made her heart and stomach roll around. She turned it one way, then another, and grunted in frustration. "Oh wow. There are no actual street names."

As Blue turned from one side to the other in the back seat, Gramma's gaze continually shifted there. And the car drifted left.

"Gramma." Pru put her hand on her shoulder. "Please. Watch the road."

"She's not happy."

"She's had a trauma, a bath, and is in a car with strangers," Pru reminded her. "You wouldn't be happy, either. Just keep your eyes on the road, and I'll watch for..." She studied the map. "A place called Hillbrook Farm."

"So is that an actual farm? Maybe it's like Waterford and they have other dogs there."

"I have no idea. It's a...place." Pru forced herself to stay calm and focused, despite the fact that the day had spiraled far out of her control. "Whatever it is, we turn left after it."

"Got it." Gramma shot her a quick look and then reached over to pat Pru's leg. "Chill, as you would say."

Pru just sighed.

"Child, we're having fun. We're doing something worthwhile and different. It's Christmas Eve, and you have to remember that sometimes life isn't quite the straight line that you had planned. That's what makes it wonderful."

Pru managed a smile and a nod, tamping down the growing sensation of dread as the snow started to slowly turn the road ahead a nice, bright, slippery white.

"Just stay focused, Gramma. Keep your eyes on the road, and we'll be fine." She peered up at the slate-gray sky and the slow, steady snowfall. Mom must be out of her mind with worry.

She grabbed her phone to see if she'd responded to the news that they found the dog's owner. She had. "Ouch."

"What did she say?" Gramma asked.

"Six—count 'em, six—angry-face emojis. All of which I totally deserve."

"You do not," Gramma shot back. "I do, but not you. Tell her this is entirely my fault and she should be mad at me, not you."

"We're both to blame," Pru said. "But I need to tell

her where we're going just in case Old Man Cutter decides to kill us."

"Prudence!"

"I'm kidding." Kind of. Swallowing that truth, she typed a text.

Mom, please don't be mad or worried. Things just didn't quite go our way. But just so you know, we're on our way to find a man named Bill Cutter, who lives ten(ish) miles northwest of Holly Hills, past a place called Hillbrook Farm. He's very distraught about losing his dog, and Gramma and I are going to make his Christmas Eve!

She hit send and put the phone away, not wanting to see the *seven* angry faces that would be the response. Plus, she had to concentrate, because the road got windy and steadily rose with the foothills as they drove into the Blue Ridge Mountains. With each mile, Gramma seemed to drive slower, making the ride seem interminable, but eventually they reached an abandoned roadside fruit stand with a faded hand-painted sign that said, *Hillbrook Buy Local Honey Here.*

"Is that Hillbrook Farm?" Pru wondered. "Should we take the next left?"

"Just tell me where to go, lass." Despite her lilting brogue, Gramma leaned a little closer to the steering wheel, practically pulling the thing into her chest now.

"You okay?" Pru asked as the weight of how dangerous this was pressed on her. "'Cause you don't have to drive, Gramma."

"Pffft. I drove a horse cart from the port all the way back to my farm in the snow." She spoke through slightly gritted teeth. "I surely can get a 2016 Toyota Avalon through the foothills in a dusting."

Pru's heart thumped with each slow turn of the tires, dread building as she peered through the windshield wipers, which were now pushing a fairly significant amount of snow. "Okay. I think I see...wait. There. There's a turn there. Looks like a driveway." Pru leaned all the way forward, squinting through snow. "Yes, that's the road. Turn. Now."

Gramma hit the brakes a little hard, and they swerved, gasped, then she righted the car and started to chug up a hill.

"Oh..." Pru pressed her hands to her chest. "This is kind of steep."

"We're fine," Gramma assured her, although her white-knuckle grip said differently.

"Is this road even paved?" It was impossible to see where they were going.

"Paved enough. How far up this hill do we go?"

Pru looked down and studied the map. "Hard to say," she admitted. "Just go straight."

"Can't." The road suddenly curved to the left, the unexpected turn making Gramma fling the wheel that way, and the backend whipped out in the other direction. In a flash of panic, Gramma smashed the brakes, which sent them spinning almost all the way around, the car skating on ice until it finally came to a stop.

They both shrieked and Blue barked, but after a second, Pru realized everything was fine...except for the two back tires hanging off of the shoulder over a ditch.

"Oh, sweet St. Patrick, I'm so sorry." Gramma closed her eyes. "That one took me by surprise."

"It's okay," Pru assured her, patting her arm, trying to calm her own beating heart and figure out how bad

it was. She turned to look out the side. *Bad.* "It's fine. We're fine. Just hit the gas and see if we can get back on the road."

She revved the accelerator, and the back wheels spun loudly in mud or ice or some combination of both.

"Try again," Pru said.

But Gramma turned to look at Blue, who'd started whimpering. "She's scared, too."

"No need to be." Pru reached to take off her seat belt. "Let me see how stuck we are."

"Saints alive," Gramma muttered, staring into the back seat. "Oh dear."

"Just let me look."

"No…it's not the car." Gramma adjusted her bifocals to get a better look. "It's the dog."

At the soft whisper of the last word, Pru followed Gramma's gaze to Blue, who'd finally settled in a corner, panting. And then she noticed the wet spot on the leather. A big, dark, gooey wet spot.

"She peed," Pru said. "She must be really scared. I'll sit with her when—"

"I don't think that's pee, child." Gramma's eyes were locked on Blue, who, for the first time, didn't look back. Instead, her head was down, focused on her bottom and belly. "Her water broke."

Oh, that's why she was restless. Pru processed this news with one simple thought: They had to get this dog home.

"I'll push the car out of the mud." She reached for the door handle and yanked it open, stepping out into the snowy cold. "You just gently hit the gas, and I'll push."

"Aye, lass. But be careful. We can call for help."

"If we have to." Or have time. "Just let me see if a little push will get us going."

But the minute she saw the right tire halfway disappeared in mud and snow, she knew she didn't have the strength to push the car up the hill. She let Gramma accelerate anyway, which shot some slush in the air and on her clothes but did nothing.

"Okay. I'll call Mom," she said, climbing back in as Gramma turned off the engine, her attention 100 percent on Blue.

"Aye, it would be good to have a vet," she said.

Pru pulled out her phone and blinked in surprise when she saw the Text Not Delivered red notification next to the last one she'd sent. Which meant Mom didn't know where she was after all.

"Aw, geez. Mom's going to be apoplectic." She re-sent the text, peering at the bars of service. No, fix that. The *zero* bars of service. "Give me your phone, Gramma."

She did and then opened her door to get in the back with Blue. Pru unlocked Gramma's phone and prayed for service. But no such luck.

She closed her eyes, hating to deliver this news. "We don't have cell service out here."

But Gramma Finnie was already in the back with Blue, stroking her head. "Then we'll have to have a litter right here in the car, won't we?"

Seriously? Could this get any worse? Pru leaned back and looked up at the sky, knowing full well that there was no end in sight to this snow. So, yes, this most certainly could get worse.

Should she leave an old woman alone in a car with

a dog in labor and walk for help? Or stay and protect them both? Pru, whose life was firmly dictated by doing the right thing, simply didn't know what the right thing was this time.

Molly slammed the Jeep door behind her, blinking up at the snow that dropped like dust on her cheeks and the tears she was about to shed.

"If it's snowing here, it's worse in Holly Hills." She squeezed her phone and stared at the screen she'd refreshed a hundred times in the last few hours. "Why isn't she answering my texts?"

"She may not have service." Trace came up behind her and wrapped both strong arms around her. "She's going to be fine, babe. They're returning the dog and coming straight home, but just in case, let's rally the troops and launch a proper search."

She sighed and turned to look up at him, letting herself lean against his chest and feel the heart she'd come to love so completely in the past year. "I'm scared, Trace."

"Shh." He tipped her chin up and looked into her eyes. "We've been through worse. And we'll go through worse. But being scared doesn't change a thing. We have the world's strongest, smartest family behind us, we have each other, and our daughter is the most responsible, mature, level-headed girl that ever walked this earth."

She managed a smile. "A miracle, considering she was conceived in the most irresponsible, immature, dizzy-headed way imaginable."

"But fun," he whispered, adding a kiss.

"That's what they were looking for," she mused, making him draw back.

"A roll in the back of a van? Sorry, but Gramma's too old, and Pru..." His eyes widened in horror. "Don't even go there for twenty years."

That made her laugh. "I told you I heard them talking in the living room."

He nodded. "Pru was upset about the wedding planner. But Gramma?"

"I didn't hear what she said, but I've been picking up vibes in our conversations. I really think she's bored and feeling her age lately."

He stroked her cheek. "So they're having a little adventure. They won't do anything stupid."

"Driving to Holly Hills on Christmas Eve was stupid."

"If that's the worst thing she does, we should count our blessings."

He was right, of course, but still she clung to him—and his faith in their daughter—as they walked back toward the kennels to find everyone and discuss the best thing to do: wait or search.

In her heart, she already knew what the Kilcannon clan would want to do. Even on Christmas Eve. Oh heck. Especially on Christmas Eve.

Shane came out of the kennels with his Staffy, Ruby, on his heels. The minute he saw her face, his easy smile faded to a worried expression on his chiseled features. "No luck?" he asked.

Molly shook her head. "And we've lost touch with her by phone."

"Dad and Garrett are back there," he said, angling

his head toward the auxiliary training field behind the kennels. "I'll get Darcy, and she'll bring Josh. Aidan and Beck are in the air on their way back from Savannah and should land at the airstrip any minute. In fact, I can send him a message to fly to Holly Hills."

It might be easier to get there by air than car. "That's a good idea," Molly said. "And everyone else?"

"Everyone's here. Liam's in the back with Genghis. Andi and the kids are already in the house baking for tonight. So are Jessie and Chloe. We'll call the Mahoneys, although Connor and Braden pulled duty at the fire station until five. Ella's probably on her way here with Aunt Colleen. Not sure if Declan's on duty, too, but he can call in to the Holly Hills station for backup."

With every word, Molly felt more of her worry lift.

"Okay," Trace said. "Let's meet in the kitchen and set up a plan."

As they rounded the kennels to get Dad and Garrett, Trace tightened his grip on Molly's arm.

"Nothing rivals the power of the Kilcannons in a crisis," he said.

She nodded, looking up at him. "Is it a crisis?" she asked, hating the lump forming in her throat.

"Not yet," he assured her. But deep inside, she knew he was as worried as she was. He was just being strong for her.

Not ten minutes later, the Waterford Farm kitchen was packed with Kilcannons. With each new arrival, Molly's heart lifted with hope. As she brought them up to speed on all she knew, Dad made coffee, filling the house's most central gathering place with a familiar and comforting aroma.

Her brothers Shane, Garrett, and Liam sat at the counter in their usual seats, but not wearing their usual relaxed expressions. Sisters-in-law Jessie and Chloe were close by, quietly finishing some of the preparations they'd been working on for tonight's family party.

Molly put her arms around both women, pressing her head to Jessie's shoulder, her friend since childhood.

"Thanks, guys," she whispered. "Gramma should be here doing this."

"Shhh." Jessie gave her a squeeze. "Everything's going to be fine, Molly."

She hoped so.

At the table, Andi sat with her son, Christian, who was anxiously picking tiny pieces of candy off the gingerbread house he'd made with Pru a few days ago, while baby Fiona slept in a carrier on the table.

"They're going to be okay, Molly," Andi said, gently taking her son's hand from the house he was going to ruin, giving him a much-needed hug of reassurance. "They're going to come walking in that door any minute."

"If not, Jag'll find them," Christian piped in, and on cue, the mighty head of his German shepherd lifted. "Right, Daddy?" he called to Liam. "Can't Jag find anyone?"

"Anyone," her brother answered. "You bet Jag can find them, Son."

"And Shane'll turn this state upside down himself if Pru or Gramma need help," Chloe whispered.

Molly felt light-headed with love for all of them. The only thing bigger than her brothers' shoulders were their hearts. And right now, those shoulders were lined up at the counter, hunched over phones, maps, and weather reports.

But then the kitchen door popped open, and human sunshine poured in.

"Molly!" Darcy, the youngest and always brightest of the clan, flew into the room, arms extended toward her sister, her two dogs at her heels. "I just read the family group text. Holly Hills? What were they thinking?" She glanced at her brothers as Kookie and Stella bounded under the table to sniff Rusty, Dad's sleeping setter.

"Did you find anything when you poked around Gramma's apartment?" Molly asked her. "Any clue what they might be doing up there?"

"Looking for old, new, borrowed, and blue things. But I didn't see anything specific."

"Is Josh coming?" Liam asked Darcy. "We need another truck."

"He's on his way." Darcy set her phone on the counter. "Aidan and Beck just texted that they filed a new flight plan and are landing at a private airfield near Holly Hills that he knows of."

Not a single Kilcannon hesitated when one was in need, Molly thought as she pulled her little sister closer and planted a kiss on Darcy's blonde head. "You're the best, Darce."

"We got this, Molls." Dad came closer, offering her a cup of coffee that was as comforting as his favorite nickname for her.

"Thanks, Dad."

He cleared his throat, and all the chatter in the room quieted. No matter how old they got, how married, independent, and grown, when this man took the center of the room, every man, woman, and child with Kilcannon blood listened.

"We can't just head off without a plan or strategy," Dad said. "And nobody should be alone. Let's break into twos and check the routes so we cover all the possibilities."

"She didn't say anything about what she was doing?" Shane asked. "Why not? That's not like Pru or Gramma Finnie."

Dad cocked his head. "My mother can be pretty spontaneous. At least, when she was younger."

"Well, Pru's not," Trace said. "It would take a pretty compelling reason for her to slide this far off track."

Molly shook her head as the gut punch of guilt hit again "But she wanted to 'own' a piece of the wedding, and I agreed—no, I encouraged her to make it a surprise." She closed her eyes against some unexpected tears. "This is all my fault for not—"

"Hush."

"Stop."

"Not your fault they took off at dawn on a day we were expecting snow."

"Don't you dare take the blame."

She looked around at her family, a rush of affection drowning out the guilt. "You're right," she agreed. "But I still don't have a clue why they'd go to Holly Hills. What's there that isn't in Bitter Bark, other than two hundred Santas and reindeer?"

"I have an idea," Dad said, snapping his fingers. "Can someone grab Gramma's laptop?"

"Got it," Darcy said, shooting up and out the door to the hall.

"Who knows her password?" Dad asked.

"I do." At least seven voices chimed in.

"If you're going to check her blog, you're in for a disappointment," Jessie said. "I keep waiting for her Christmas entry, and she hasn't made it yet."

"I think she has writer's block," Andi added from the table. "She made a comment the other day when I picked Fiona up."

Molly nodded in agreement. "I think that's the root cause of all her restlessness. She has writer's block."

"She has life block," Dad said, making them all look at him. "I've sensed a real restlessness in her that I remember from when my father died."

When Darcy came zooming back in, she already had the laptop open and on. "Is it wrong if we check her internet history, Dad?" she asked.

"It's wrong if we don't," he said, clicking keys.

Molly exchanged a bittersweet smile with Trace. "I know what you're thinking," she said.

"The fact that your grandmother *has* an internet history is what makes her so special," he replied. "One of the many things."

She leaned her head on his shoulder, forcing herself to think of other clues. "Where would they go for something old, new, borrowed, or blue?"

"Okay," Dad said, his attention on the screen. "Her last search was 'jewelry repair.'"

Molly inched closer. "That makes sense for something old. Anything in Holly Hills?"

"Yep. One called Emerald Isle Jewelers."

"That sounds like the one Gramma Finnie would pick," Garrett said.

"Give me the number. I'll call them right now." Darcy grabbed her phone as Dad read her the phone number, walking out of the kitchen to make the call in the quiet of the dining room.

"Don't forget the dog," Trace said, putting his hand on Molly's shoulder. "They're returning a lost, pregnant dog to her owner."

Every person in the room turned to stare at him.

"No one mentioned that," Liam said dryly.

Molly and Trace shared a guilty look. "We forgot," she admitted. "But somehow, they found out who the dog belongs to, and they were going about ten miles or so out of town to return her."

Liam and Shane stood at the same time. "We need to get up there and fan out."

"And someone needs to go to the jewelry store," Darcy said, coming back into the room. "They dropped off a pin to be repaired and were supposed to pick it up, but they haven't shown up yet, and they're closing soon."

"Okay, now we have a plan," Dad said. "Let's break into groups and go."

As they coordinated that, Molly took one more sip of coffee and closed her eyes.

"Feel better?" Trace whispered. "We have a direction now. And a posse."

She barely smiled. "I'll feel better once those two are back in my arms, and not a minute before."

Chapter Eleven

A s the car got colder and the dog got deeper into her labor, Pru really questioned her decision to stay. Not that taking that hand-drawn map and powering through the snowfall on foot to find Bill Cutter made any sense, but at least she'd have done *something*. But if that something had been leaving Gramma Finnie in this car alone while Pru trudged through unfamiliar terrain and knocked on the door of a complete stranger, then staying was the right decision. Cold, worrisome, and unfortunate, but right.

Of course, they were safer and stronger together, and someone *might* come along the road and see them. Too bad they didn't get stuck in a ditch on the main road, where they'd be visible to anyone driving by— not that they'd heard a single car in the time they'd been sitting here. They were just far enough away from the road and around a corner that someone would have to be looking for them to find them.

However, if Pru knew the Kilcannons, someone *would* be looking for them, especially now that she'd been unable to reach Mom for hours. That's why she'd walked up the road and tied her red Christmas scarf to the tree branch at the turn, hoping Mom would see it.

While they waited, it got colder and snowier, and poor Blue hadn't stopped panting except to whimper and adjust herself on the back seat. Pru had found one old blanket in the trunk, which Gramma refused to wrap up in. Instead, she laid it out on the back seat between them, creating an extremely makeshift whelping box. They'd scared up some hand sanitizer and a basic first aid kit, which would be quite useful if Blue needed a Band-Aid, sterile eye patch, or some ibuprofen.

But Pru wasn't too worried about Blue. She and Gramma both had seen plenty of litters born, and most of the time it was just a long process, but not painful or dangerous. Blue didn't really even need their help unless something weird went wrong. Hopefully, Mom and Trace would show up soon, and this whole "adventure" could come to an end. Along with Pru's allowance for a year, but she had that coming.

She checked her phone again, which still had no service and, darn, almost no battery as the phone exhausted itself searching for a signal. She turned it off, tried Gramma Finnie's, which had about the same amount of battery and no service, either.

"Mom must have lost her mind by now."

"Mmm. She'll get over it." Gramma stroked Blue's head again, but the dog sort of shook her off, clearly not wanting any affection.

"I hope she's over it by the wedding," Pru said glumly. "So much for the somethings, huh? We'll be lucky if we get to *go* to the wedding. We'll be the something missing."

Gramma Finnie snorted a quick laugh. "They can't ground me."

Pru gave her a look. "They'll take your keys."

She didn't seem fazed, but concentrated on the dog. "Donchya be worried, lass."

"Who? Me or the dog?"

"Both of you." Her smile was not quite as wide and warm as it had been two hours earlier. She tucked herself deeper into her down jacket and tried not to shiver, which just broke Pru's heart.

"Take the blanket, Gramma."

She shook her head. "Blue needs it. It's comforting her."

Pru exhaled into her cupped hands and rubbed them together. "I'm going to go down to the road again. Flagging someone is our only hope."

"You tried five times already, and there hasn't been a car."

"Sixth time's the charm." She grabbed the handle, but Gramma reached over Blue and pressed on Pru's jacket.

"Look. We're gettin' one. I want you here with me."

Pru looked down to see Blue's distended belly suddenly grow huge and hard, then contract into a tight ball. The dog dropped her head down between her legs and went completely silent.

Five minutes passed, maybe more, but slowly, very, very slowly, a dark wet lump emerged from her, spilling out onto the blanket, completely cocooned in a thin, transparent sac.

"Oh!" Gramma and Pru made the sound at exactly the same time as they were able to make out the puppy's head, not much bigger than Pru's thumb, and its itty-bitty legs.

It was all black, or at least looked that way now, and utterly still. Blue stared at her puppy like an alien had just fallen from the sky, inching her nose closer, then jerked back, startled by the very scent of it.

Pru cracked up at the reaction, and Gramma Finnie shook her head and tsked noisily. "You'll get used to it, Blue. Go on now, lass. Give your baby a lick. Break that sac."

As if she understood exactly what Gramma was saying, Blue leaned close again and stroked her tongue over the puppy's head, and the second time, the sheer sac split open. Out popped the little head, eyes glued shut, fur glistening. Blue kept licking until the tiny creature was completely free and started to roll into the crack between the seat cushion and the back.

"Oh no ye don't, wee one." Gramma expertly slipped her hand under the body, cupping it around the puppy, cooing to Blue with gentle, encouraging sounds. "Let's give you an Irish blessing, puppy." She raised it slightly, holding the tiny, mewing creature with tender hands. "'May strong arms hold you, caring hearts tend you, and may love await you at every step.'"

"That's what you said to Fiona," Pru said with a smile.

"Aye, and when you were born, lass."

Blue settled into a different position, her mesmerizing gaze on the puppy, then Gramma, as if giving permission to help out with number one while they waited for number two.

"Any idea how long before the next one?" Pru asked. "I think I should turn the car on and try to warm that little thing up a bit."

Gramma nodded. "Do that, please, and I'll try to put him in the blanket."

"You sure it's a him?"

"Not yet, but I don't want to poke this little body. We'll find out soon enough."

"Name?" Pru asked.

"Well, we have Blue. Let's call this little something Borrowed."

Pru gave a dry laugh. "Oh, this is so not what Mom had in mind when she gave us this job. But I like the way you think, Gramma. Think there will be four?"

"There could be two, four, or fourteen."

"Oh God." Climbing into the driver's seat, Pru turned on the ignition and switched up the heat. It didn't help much, but it took the chill out of the car after a moment. "Gramma, what will we do with them all? We're going to have to find Bill Cutter or at least call the sheriff. Something."

"We'll figure it out, child. Borrowed is breathing fine and not fussing, so let's count that blessing."

"Okay, I'll go try the street again, then we'll just wait." Pru let out a sigh. "I have never in my life been in so much trouble."

"Oh, I have," Gramma said with a quick laugh. "It's kind of fun."

Pru turned and stared at her. "I don't think it's fun to be in trouble."

Her blue eyes glinted. "It is for the right reasons."

"What do you mean?"

"You go stand on the road for two minutes, no longer. See if that red scarf is still there, then hurry back, child."

Pru sensed there was more to this list of instructions. "And then?"

She sighed. "Then I'll tell you how I got that pin back and why some trouble is worth getting into."

Pru couldn't wait.

Spring was in the air, and County Wexford was awash with green that May of 1946. The kind of green that hurts your eyes and heart. The kind of green that seeps under your skin and gives you hope. The kind of green that makes a fifteen-year-old girl want to climb on a horse and ride bareback over the hills in search of love and her first kiss.

But sadly, Finola Brennan wasn't climbing anything but the hayloft that fine green afternoon, tossing down bales to the livestock below, a hymn still in her head from yesterday's Mass. The closest she could get to the green hills today was a glimpse of the grass outside through the space left by a few missing wood boards in the wall.

There, she could see Da hard at work with a shovel in his hands, digging a trough for the new pigs that were just born. Edward and Jack had just ridden off in the cart to join Patrick in the north pasture, leaving her with the hay bales.

But what she really wanted was to be out there. On a sigh, she settled on a bale and leaned over to suck in some spring air and stare at the hills just as the silhouette of a man appeared on the crest of one. She stared at him, taking in the long, easy strides of the stranger, unable to look away as he got closer and closer. He wore a cotton shirt, suspenders, and trousers and the strangest-looking flat cap she'd ever seen. It looked more like a soldier's hat.

"What do ye want?" Da called out to him, making Finnie suck in a surprised breath. He was normally so hospitable to guests, and strangers, too.

"I'm looking for a lass named Finola Brennan. I've been told this is her home."

Another gasp, but this time Finnie slapped her hand over her mouth to silence herself. He wanted her? The man came closer, and while his face was still in shadow, she could certainly make out his fine form, lanky and lean, but no lad, for sure.

"Have you now?" Her father leaned on his shovel, no hand extended as the young man came closer. From this angle, she couldn't see his face at all, but she recognized the hat now. British Army. But that was no British tongue he was speaking. That was an Irishman.

So she understood why Da was so ice cold.

He'd no love for the Irish boys who'd snuck off to fight the war. In his opinion, they were all complicit in the tragic death of her sister. Not that his thinking made a lick of sense, since not only had one had Vi's heart when she ran away to London, but Timothy was with her when a German bomb took out the boarding house where she lived.

Fact was, Vi went off to London to help the war effort and save lives, and it mattered not that some of her Irish menfolk had done the same. If not one single

Irishman had decided to fight—and it turned out that nearly four thousand of them had—Vi would still have gotten on that boat that chilly December morn.

And she still would have died in the rubble next to Timothy Donovan.

It was the Germans, defeated and miserable, whom her father should hate. But since Vi died? Mammy and Da hated *everyone*.

"Is she here, sir?"

Finnie pushed down on her knees to get a better look just as the young man reached the split-rail fence. He stopped there, slowly took off his hat, and looked past her father to the barn and the house.

And Finnie's heart just about stopped dead in her chest.

"Seamus Kilcannon," she whispered. "As I live and breathe."

"I have something to return to her, sir." His voice floated up through the air, much deeper than she remembered, but still strong and sure. She'd heard that voice in her head a thousand times. Every night since she'd come home from the port, she'd fall asleep and think of the lad who went to war with her pin. Had he made it? Had he lived? Had he ever thought of her again?

Obviously, he had. A thrill unlike anything she'd ever known pulsed through her body, making her feel like she'd suddenly come back to life. Since Vi died, the world had been gray and brown and sad and miserable. But today seemed brighter. And now? She itched to run down there and throw herself into his arms, but—

"I have this pin, sir." He held out his hand to give

something to her father, while Finnie pressed her fists to her lips.

He has Vi's pin. Her heart literally soared, flying around her chest like a dove over cliffs. He had the pin and brought it back to her! She scrambled to her feet, barely able to rise fast enough. Seamus Kilcannon had come back, and he'd brought the very pin she'd given him!

Her head spinning so fast it made her dizzy, Finnie lifted her work skirt and threw herself onto the loft ladder, slipping twice as she rushed to get down. She hit the ground, tripped over a hay bale, and righted herself, running to the door and around the front of the barn.

"Get out of here!"

At Da's ferocious command, she froze. Then, silent, she peeked around the side of the barn to watch the exchange in horror.

"Never come back here, do ye understand?" Da's voice rose and cracked, and Seamus backed up, but didn't look shocked. Her father wasn't the only Irishman who didn't like the young ones who'd broken with the country's neutrality.

"I wanted to return Finola's pin."

"Never say her name!" her father shouted. "And this?" He raised his hand, presumably holding the pin. "This isn't hers! Go now. Get far away."

Da didn't wait for a response, but spun on one booted foot and marched toward the house without noticing Finnie hiding around the corner. He made it halfway to the house and stopped, holding up his two hands with the pin between them, reminding her of the priest raising the communion host.

But there was no reverence in this move. Nothing at all holy in the dark curses he let out. He ripped his hands apart with a violent jerk, throwing the pieces to the ground on either side of his boots.

And Finnie's heart broke right along with the precious pin.

She stayed stone-still as he strode into the house, his boots making the whole front porch quake. As soon as he was inside, she raced to the spot, dropped to her knees, and smashed her hand on the ground in search of the last bit of Mary Violet she might ever have left.

Almost instantly, the pin pricked her palm, and she grabbed the broken piece, lifting it to see he'd cracked off one of the shamrocks. Was the other one—

"Finola?"

She turned slowly at the sound of the young man's voice, meeting an intense gaze that, like before, seemed to slice right through her. He was so different, yet still the same.

"Seamus," she whispered. "You'd best leave."

"No."

She blinked at him.

"I want to talk to you."

In spite of the May sunshine, chills blossomed up her arms, making the hair on the back of her neck stand up. It was like every night when she'd close her eyes and try to tell herself a story to go to sleep, like Vi used to. She'd make up a place and a person...but it was always Seamus in those still-awake story dreams.

But in her imagination, he looked like a scared lad trying to run away to war. Not like this. Not a young man with whiskers and shoulders and the hint of a sly smile.

She glanced at the house, half afraid Da would come back out. "Up the road. To the east. Under the alder tree. Wait for me."

He nodded once, put his cap back on, and left, half running across the grass as if he, too, expected to be stopped by Paddy Brennan.

While she waited for him to disappear, Finnie searched the grass for the broken shamrock, but couldn't find it. After a few minutes, she stood and made a decision she somehow knew would change her life.

Without so much as a glance over her shoulder, she took off, practically leaping over a hay bale, throwing the gate open, and running full force up the first hill toward the road. She looked back once as she ran down the other side, to make sure she couldn't be seen from the house, and only then did she slow to a trot.

By the time she reached the alder tree, she'd almost caught her breath. But when she saw Seamus Kilcannon sitting under it, his cap low, a long piece of grass in his mouth, she was breathless again.

"Ye kept yer promise," she whispered.

He slid the hat off and grinned up at her, and his handsome face came to light. He was a strong-boned young man with dancing eyes and charming lips that made her think of one thing only.

"Now I want that kiss, lass."

That was the one thing.

He stood, surprising her with his great height. Oh yeah, war had changed him. "Took me nigh on two years to find you, Finola."

He'd looked for her since the war ended? She nearly swayed. "I thought maybe…"

"I made it," he said simply.

"How did you…" She lifted the broken pin still clutched in her hand. "Did you look for this for two years, too?"

"Never sold it." He took a few steps closer, forcing her to look up. Way up. She was a small girl, and he was…not small. "I got back to the cart vendor, the one where you'd been. He took pity on me and bought my lamp. I went back to return the pin, but you'd been long gone."

Oh, why had she rushed away from the port?

So she could have this moment, she supposed.

"I thought it was a sign I had to keep the pin for luck, so I did." He gave a smile that tripped her heart. Maybe broke it. "Kept it in my pocket wrapped in your little lace kerchief from the time I got on the boat until today."

She felt her jaw loosen at the admission. "You did? All that time?"

"See?" He pulled the bit of linen and lace from his pocket. "I don't know who has the initials MVB, but I've rubbed my fingers on the stitches a thousand times."

"'Twas my sister's. I stitched it."

"Then I've touched you, once removed." He held the kerchief out to her. "It brought me luck, it did."

Bought him luck and brought her…him. "'Tis fortunate, then."

"I took three bullets, fell out of a train, and damn near drowned savin' a man's life. Got home, and some folk hate me, but my father's always sick, so it looks like my mam will let me back in the family glassblowin' business. They say the Waterford company is getting back into it now, as well. Could be a good thing down here in the South."

She nodded slowly, taking in all this news about this new person who'd fallen from heaven and landed on her farm. "Are ye far?"

"Not too. I can meet you here, Finola, once in a blue moon. Perhaps more."

"I'm fifteen," she said, lifting her chin as if to defy her very age.

"I'm eighteen," he replied.

"I've never even been kissed."

There was that smile again, making the sun shine and the birds sing and one poor lass melt into the green, green grass. "I aim to fix that, Finola Brennan."

"Do you now?"

He tucked his finger under her chin and raised it so their gazes met. "I never forgot your kindness, lass. Never forgot your sweet blue eyes or your spirit when you gave me that pin."

She tried to swallow, but it was impossible. In one hand, her fingers closed over the pin. In the other, she crushed the kerchief.

"And I swore if I ever got back in one piece, I'd find you and make you mine."

"I was a child."

He winked at her. "Not one now."

No, she'd be sixteen in a few months. What could Da say then? Girls her age got married all the time, or in a year.

"Then I'll see you tomorrow, Finola Brennan."

He leaned down, closed the space between them, and barely brushed her lips with his, but it was enough for her knees to weaken and toes to curl in her boots. Without another word, he stepped away and headed toward the next hill, surrounded by light and green and hope for a better, brighter life.

It didn't matter what her father threatened. Nothing mattered. She reached up and lightly pressed the kerchief he'd stroked a thousand times to her lips.

Something deep inside told her that Seamus Kilcannon would kiss her lips a thousand times in this life, and every kiss would be better than the one before.

Chapter Twelve

"Aye. 'Tis better than the one before."

Pru had to shake her head to come back to the present moment, since Gramma Finnie's story had taken her far away across the miles and the years. "What is?"

"The puppies, lass. We've got three now."

And Pru had been so lost on the farm in County Wexford, she'd barely noticed Blue had given birth to two more pups. She forced herself to focus on the wet mess of newborns and afterbirth all over the back seat and not the green hills of Ireland and Gramma Finnie and Grandpa Seamus's first kiss.

But they weren't in County Wexford under an alder tree. They were in a freezing car with a dog still in labor, the blanket between them covered in blood, mucus, and afterbirth, and three very tiny puppies crying and whining so much it was like a newborn symphony in that car. They had no cell phone service, no way to move the car, and no real chance of walking for help now.

Pru had to let go of the past to take care of this messy present. "Are we sure there are more?" she asked.

"Most certainly," Gramma said, gently rubbing Blue's belly. "At least one, maybe two. She's gettin' tired."

Pru studied the dog for a moment. She was still panting and whimpering, but didn't seem as shocked by what was happening to her. The puppies hadn't nursed yet, but they were snuggling close to her and getting ready.

"I never watched a birth when we didn't know exactly how many were in there," Pru said, thinking of the many times her mother had been called for minor problems when Pru was little and couldn't be left alone. She'd spent more than a few nights at the vet office in town, watching animals give birth.

"Could it be breech?" she asked, knowing that was the most common problem.

Gramma looked up with genuine concern. "I was thinkin' that could be the issue now. Let's look at her."

They carefully repositioned Blue on her back and spread her back legs, and Pru squinted at the poor pooch's privates. "I think I see a paw pad."

"Oh, sweet St. Patrick. One of us has to go in there." Gramma Finnie gave a sly smile and tapped her nose. "Nose goes."

Pru laughed softly. "Why do I teach you these things?"

"So I can be young and carefree like you." There was a bittersweet note in her voice, enough that Pru looked up again and studied her great-grandmother's weathered features. "Does talking about Grandpa Seamus make you sad?"

"Of course not, lass. It makes me feel old, though. Like I'm surely at the end."

No! That was the whole reason they'd come on this adventure. "Well, it gives me hope," Pru said quickly. "And I want to hear every single detail."

Gramma's eyes widened imperceptibly. "Not every one." Then she leaned closer. "Gives you hope for what?"

"That a boy will kiss me under a tree like that."

She gave a soft hoot. "Lass, your mother, your grandmother, and your great-grandmother did a whole lot more than kissin', as you know. Truth of the matter is that you come from a long line of women who should not have worn white. Each one of us already in the family way when we said 'I do.'"

Pru chuckled. "I'm going to break that streak."

"Ye better. Just like you better haul out the rest of the hand sanitizer and get a couple of fingers up in Blue."

She grunted. "I've never turned a breech pup, but I've seen my mother do it, and I've heard her walk people through it on the phone."

"And you're smart and capable."

Pru knew buttering up when she heard it. "But what an experience. Maybe you should do it, Gramma."

She thought for a moment, then shook her head. "I will if you want me to, child, but I feel your fingers are longer, stronger, and younger. She needs you."

Pru knew her great-grandmother well enough to realize that was no excuse. It was what was best for the dog, and that was how Kilcannons rolled.

She nodded solemnly, reaching for the nearly empty purse-sized bottle of hand sani and dribbling some out, rubbing her hands while making the face of concentration she'd seen on her mother and grandfather, the two best vets in the world.

"Did you see Grandpa Seamus the next day?" she asked softly.

For a second, Gramma didn't answer. Then she sighed. "Aye. And most days after that. Two fingers would be best, lass."

Pru nodded and slid them in, cringing at the slimy insides of the dog. Blue turned her head and looked up at Gramma Finnie as if she could help her out of this bind.

"Hush, sweet one." Gramma took the dog's face in her two hands with comfort and enough strength to keep her from snapping at any discomfort.

Pru couldn't see a thing, so she just closed her eyes and imagined the outline of one of these tiny puppies. Was that the one foot she felt? Yes, it had to be a paw. "I have it. Just one, though."

"Get it out," Gramma encouraged her. "Just slide it out real slow and simple, and then you'll have to reposition the pup."

Pru blew out a breath. "If I can't do that, she'll need a C-section."

"And that is beyond our ken, lass."

"No kidding." Pru managed to get another finger in and use it to slide from one side to the other, searching for the dog's hock to straighten the tiny leg. "Come on, kiddo. Help me out here."

"'Tis so wee," Gramma said, eyeing the pups. "And they're getting cold."

This was definitely going from an adventure to big fat trouble in a hurry. But she couldn't find that tiny joint, and if she didn't and this pup pushed through, it could be born with a broken leg.

"Wait, wait, I think I—"

"What do you think you're doing?" The shout was accompanied by a loud bang and a bump so hard it shook the car.

Gramma and Pru both gasped, but Blue started flailing—enough that the pup went right back up the canal.

"Get your hands off Queenie!" A man stood outside the car, wiping snow off Pru's window with one hand and giving another good smack with the front end of a rifle.

"I think Bill Cutter found us," Pru muttered, withdrawing her hand.

Gramma let go of the dog, who managed to right herself and look up at her master, letting out one bark before resuming her birth position. But that pup was not going to come out without some help. At least, it would not come out safely.

"Open the door!" he insisted with a gravelly voice, then bent down to reveal an old and weathered face, bloodshot eyes, and wild gray hair and a beard.

"Think he'll shoot us?" Pru asked, staring at him. Sadly, the question wasn't a joke, and from the look on Gramma's face, she knew that. Her expression turned stern and serious and, yes, a little angry.

She leaned down to deliver that anger to the new arrival. "There are puppies in here, and the cold air could kill 'em," she hollered. "And the next one's breech, which could kill the dog. Can you push the car out, please?"

For a long time, the man was silent. Freakishly, dead silent. Then he walked to the back of the car.

"Should I go up and turn on the ignition?" Pru asked.

The only answer was a whimper and moan from Blue. Gramma held her closer. "We got to birth this pup, and that man can help us, go straight to hell, or shoot us both."

"I'll take door number one."

Just then, the window behind Gramma Finnie darkened with the figure of the man again. This time, when he cleared the snow, they saw his face first and not the gun.

"I can't push you out."

"Then get help," Pru yelled. "Now!"

Without a word, he disappeared, and Gramma notched her chin toward the dog. "Turn the pup, lass, or I will."

With a slow inhale, Pru inserted three fingers into Blue and tried again, but she just couldn't get hold of the pup. Sweat dribbled down her back, and her whole body trembled with how much she wanted to save this puppy and Blue.

Mom could do this. Mom could do this in her sleep. "What was I thinking?" Pru murmured.

"Hush." Gramma pressed her palm against Pru's cheek, but the powder-soft parchment of her skin was ice cold. Instead of feeling the comfort she was trying to offer, Pru was reminded that this car was stuck, they were freezing, the pups could all die, and there was a guy with a rifle out there. And Gramma was darn near ninety.

"I should never have left," Pru whispered, letting the guilt rise up and strangle her. "Never should have gone against what I always do."

"And you did it for me." Gramma's voice cracked. "I'm sorry."

Pru shook her head, partially in frustration as the pup eluded her and Blue whimpered in agony. But also because this wasn't Gramma Finnie's fault.

"I...can't...do...it." She closed her eyes and grunted in frustration. "I just don't have the strength. I don't have it."

Gramma leaned closer to whisper, "Great work isn't performed by strength, but by perseverance."

Count on Gramma for a motivational quote. But it worked. She took another breath and tried again.

But nothing changed. The pup was stuck, bass-ackward, as Uncle Shane would say, and too big to come through. Still, nature didn't care what position the pup was in. Contractions pushed it down, and with each centimeter, Blue tore and bled.

Pru closed her eyes against tears, and while she did, she heard Gramma whisper a prayer for help. When she opened her eyes, she saw a dark shadow of a man coming toward the car once again, barely visible through the snow on the windshield.

"Grizzly Adams is back," Pru groaned.

"He better have help."

Letting go of the dog, Pru put her leg through the space between the seats to get in the driver's seat. She flipped on the ignition and used the wipers to clear the windshield. "No backup, but he's got an armful of blankets, which beat the heck out of a rifle. I'm going to put the window down."

"All right."

"What should I tell him?"

"The truth. These puppies are freezing. The last one is coming out wrong. And Blue is going to die if we don't do something."

Very slowly, Pru pressed the button to lower the window. She'd honestly never been so scared in her whole life.

Molly might as well have taken a roller coaster to Holly Hills instead of the Waterford Jeep, that's how many ups and downs her heart experienced on the seemingly endless ride into the foothills and deeper into the mountains. When they arrived, the Kilcannon clan hit the small town like a rock in a pond, their ripples spreading from Main Street to the outskirts.

Garrett and Liam took the east side of town, while Jessie and Andi took Christian and the baby to see some decorations and scope the place for any sign of Gramma and Pru. Darcy and Josh headed west, and Chloe, Shane, and Dad walked up and down the pedestrian-only streets, checking out restaurants and shops. Molly and Trace took the lead clue and beelined to Emerald Isle Jewelers, just in time to meet face-to-face with an older man on the other side of the glass, locking the front door.

"We're closed," he called out, running a hand over his bald head as if he was a little sorry to turn away the business.

"We just need to ask you a quick question," Molly shouted through the glass. "I'm looking for my daughter. Did she come in here?"

He lifted his shoulder to shrug, then looked from Trace to Molly and back. "With a broken pin?"

Molly had no idea what they'd come in with.

"Maybe. She has long dark hair, kind of green-brown eyes. A little shorter than me?"

"The shamrock pin?"

Something clicked in Molly's memory, long ago and far away. Yes, Gramma had a broken pin with a shamrock. Her mother had told her a story once, about how it helped Gramma meet Grandpa Seamus.

"That has to be it," she said, looking anxiously at Trace.

The man shook his head. "I tried calling her. I can't fix that pin, not without ordering a new shamrock. Tell her to come and pick it up, or she'll have to wait until January."

Trace stepped closer to the door. "Sir, our daughter is missing. Do you have any idea where she went after she left here?"

His eyes flashed with instant sympathy, maybe a father or grandfather himself. Without answering, he unlocked the dead bolt and inched the glass door open. "Missing?" He frowned at the word. "I tried to call the number she left, and so did Angela, who works here. We wondered why she didn't come back for the pin."

And that roller coaster dropped again, taking Molly's heart for another ride.

As if he sensed that, Trace put his arm around her. "She was with an older woman," he said. "Her great-grandmother."

"And a dog," Molly added. "She told me they found a stray and then she found the owner and was going to return it. That's when we lost track of her."

"No dogs in here. Our policy is not to let them in."

"But she came in here and showed someone the pin?" Molly urged.

"I spoke with her myself and told her I'd try and find a shamrock that would work, but I couldn't. I can get the pin for you. It's in the case." He invited them in with a quick gesture, opening the door wider.

Frustration seized her. She didn't want the pin. She wanted Pru. "That's okay, we'll—"

"We'll take the pin," Trace added. At Molly's look, he said, "It's obviously important to her and Gramma Finnie. We should get it for them."

Her heart softened at how thoughtful he was, even when they were upset with Pru.

"Hang on one second." The jeweler hustled around the glass counter filled with necklaces and rings. "It's an unusual piece," he said as Molly and Trace went closer. "Not easily fixed, either. Let's see now. Here it is. Prudence Kilcannon?"

"Yes, that's her. Thank you." Trace took the envelope and handed it to Molly, who clutched it to her chest, wishing it were Pru.

"I'm sure you'll find her soon," the man said. "Holly Hills isn't a big town. Lots of tourists, yes, but no crime. So much to see. Have you checked Santa's Workshop? They might be right down on North Pole Lane this very minute."

Molly shook her head, knowing Pru would never linger over a Christmas display when her parents were this upset. It just went against everything she knew about her daughter—and Gramma Finnie.

She just knew in her heart and soul that something was very, very wrong. And she had no idea where to go next.

Chapter Thirteen

B ill Cutter was definitely a man of few words.

From the moment he returned to the car with armloads of blankets and towels and silently wrapped every puppy in one, he didn't offer a single word of explanation to Gramma Finnie or Pru. With a remarkable combination of efficiency and tenderness—and dead silence—he placed the bundles in their arms, giving the two "older" pups to Gramma and the last one to Pru. Finally, he wrapped Blue and scooped the whimpering dog into his arms with the quiet strength she'd seen Liam use when lifting a ninety-pound German shepherd.

Even with the blanket, blood dripped from Blue, terrifying Pru that maybe the last puppy, and even sweet Blue, might not make it.

Finally, he bent over to look inside the car at them. "Angels. Come."

Did he call them angels? Gramma's look echoed the question—and managed to ask a few more. *He thinks we're angels? Or is he just crazy?*

Gramma and Pru stared at each other. Should they stay? Go? Run? Risk their lives or the dogs'? What was the right thing to do? When they didn't follow him, he bent down again.

"Please, angels."

With that single word, he walked away and started hauling the dog up the hill, leaving Gramma and Pru holding three squeaky, whimpering, freezing pups in blankets.

"Did he call us…"

"Angels," Gramma confirmed. "'Tis the season for them."

Pru sat frozen—literally and figuratively—in the driver's seat. "Gramma, we can't. We don't know him. He could hurt us. You might not even make it up that hill. We can't leave the car and just follow a stranger." It all went against everything Pru had ever known or done, and each realization ratcheted up her paralyzing horror. "We just can't—"

"We can't let these puppies die," Gramma said, her voice stern and unwavering. "Come on, Pru. The adventure is over. Now we have a job to do. You heard the man. He thinks we're angels. Let's act like it."

Pru swallowed. "I'm scared, Gramma."

She reached out a chilled and knotted hand and touched Pru's face. "Don't be scared. I have a good feeling about this."

Well, Pru didn't. Trusting Gramma, she pushed out of the seat, careful to squeeze the puppy in her arms, Pru pushed up. "Okay," she muttered, her voice thick. "This time you're in charge, Gramma. I'm not as mature as I've been pretending to be."

"And I'm not as reckless."

Pru lifted a brow. "Fearless, Gramma Finnie. You are fearless, not reckless."

They climbed onto the crunchy snow, and Pru used her hip to close the car doors, not even bothering to lock them. They trudged side by side behind the mountain man carrying a dog whose blood dripped into the snow.

Pru kept her pace slow, somehow staying with Gramma but not losing sight of their guide.

In less than five minutes, he stopped, rounded a grouping of trees, and continued along what was probably a path, but it was currently covered with several inches of snow. They were past the foothills now, into the mountains, and deep into woods.

This was like a bad, bad fairy tale, only there was no prince, good queen, or happy ending in sight. Still, they stayed close behind him, pine trees brushing their coats as they navigated their way farther into the thick darkness. The snow-covered world smelled like cold and pine, as icy as the snowflakes that hit their faces and hid their trail.

How would anyone ever find them? Pru literally felt herself sway as her head grew dizzy with fear, and that sickening sensation of danger seeped hot adrenaline into her blood.

How was Gramma so cool about this? She trudged on, holding her puppies, not even slipping in her little granny boots. Right at that moment, Pru had never loved her more. Never realized how strong and noble and truly powerful that little old lady was.

"I want to be just like you," Pru whispered. "When I'm eighty-seven, I want to be you."

Without turning her head, Gramma let a slow smile pull at her lips. "'Tis a lot of time until that season, child."

Pru caught the sentiment, but heard a breathless note she didn't like. "Uh, excuse me, sir? Mr. Cutter, sir?"

He didn't stop or turn.

"Are we almost there? Because my great-grandmother is closer to ninety than eighty."

Gramma Finnie huffed. "I'm fine."

"And I'm only fourteen," she added.

He didn't say a word.

"Yesterday, we were moanin' about our ages," Gramma whispered under her breath. "Today, you're throwin' numbers around like they can save our lives."

"I just want him to have pity on us, the old and the young."

Gramma snorted. "He called us angels, lass. Never you mind. We're doin' the right thing."

She sure hoped so, because if she actually came out of this alive, Mom and Trace would probably kill her. She didn't even want to think about what Mom might be going through right now. The whole family.

"We're almost there," the man called out.

"Almost where?" Pru fought the whine in her voice, but it came out anyway.

"You'll see."

Oh God. That did not sound good.

Still standing in the doorway of Emerald Isle Jewelers, Trace took Molly's hands, gently easing them to his chest. "Think, babe. You're *sure* she didn't mention where she was going while they waited for this pin to be fixed?"

"She said..." Molly squeezed her eyes shut and, for the twentieth time, tried to replay the brief phone conversation, clinging to Trace's strong grip as she dug into her memory banks. She'd been angry and scared and hadn't listened to Pru. "They were going to get the dog cleaned up!" Her eyes popped open as she remembered. "That's what she said."

"Then they went to Melanie's place," the jeweler said. "It's called Squeaky Clean K-9s, and it's right around the corner on Mistletoe Road. If they're still open, they might know more."

"Dog groomers probably know the owner of the dog they found," Trace said, already pulling her away. "And will know where they went. Come on."

"Hurry," the man said. "The Elf Parade is starting, so everyone's closing up early for Christmas Eve."

Once again, Molly's heart soared like a roller-coaster car chugging up the track. She thanked the man with a spontaneous hug and wished him a merry Christmas, then clung to hope and Trace as they navigated the crowded streets full of tourists and holiday cheer.

But it was nearly impossible to move, as legions of green-hatted elves snaked from one side of the street to the other, tossing candy and calling out to the crowd. A jolly old St. Nick came marching down the sidewalk, his arms locked with not one but two Mrs. Clauses, along with way too many grown men wearing reindeer hats and bright red noses.

Carols blared from invisible speakers, only slightly louder than the blood rushing in Molly's ears, while thousands of lights blurred and danced as more tears filled her vision.

But nothing stopped Trace. Not the Santa with two wives, or dozens of elves, or slightly inebriated Rudolfs. He squeezed Molly's hand and threaded the obstacles like…like…well, like a man determined to find his missing daughter.

For the first time since Trace showed up on her doorstep, Molly realized exactly why God gave kids two parents. She could not have handled this, but he would carry her over that parade if he had to, and she loved him so much, she started to cry all over again.

"Come on." He tugged her along, oblivious to her meltdown of affection for him. "I see Mistletoe Road."

When they rounded the corner, they found the groomers…and a big old Closed sign on the front door.

"Ugh!" Molly dropped her head back as her heart hit bottom again.

She could feel the same frustration vibrate through Trace, who whipped his head left and right and practically sniffed out a solution to the problem like the service dogs he trained. Then her gaze moved to a flyer in the front window with four dogs and phone numbers under each, landing on a border collie with one brown eye and one blue one. Instantly, Pru's words came back to her.

Oh, Mom, this dog is so cute…She's a border, with one blue and one brown eye…

"That's it." Molly pointed to the dog. "That's the dog they found. Named Queenie. We better…" Her voice trailed off. "Why isn't there a phone number?" she practically wailed as she scanned the page, trying to figure out why the dog owner had no number.

"There's a name," Trace said, leaning closer. "William Cutter. We just have to find William Cutter." Once again, he turned and peered into the crowds lined up on either side of the street. "There."

"You found him?" she gasped.

"Someone who might know." He pointed to a jolly-looking woman with long silver-streaked black hair tumbling from a Santa hat, waving her hand to guide people to open spaces along the parade route. "Town volunteers know everyone."

Knowing that was true in Bitter Bark, Molly seized this new hope as they made their way over and Trace went right up to the woman.

"Excuse me," he said. "Do you happen to know where William Cutter lives?"

She drew back, frowning and fighting a surprised laugh. "The nutcase up on the mountain?"

Nutcase? That didn't sound good.

"Where does he live exactly?" Trace demanded.

She shook her head. "Can't rightly say, as I don't think anyone's ever dared go to his house. You sure you want to?"

"My daughter and her great-grandmother may be returning his dog to him." He glanced over his shoulder toward the grooming business. "Queenie? She has—"

"Really bizarre eyes. Yeah, that's his dog and the only reason he comes into town, but we all sort of keep a wide berth around him, if you get my drift."

Molly did not *want* to get that drift. "Is he dangerous?" she asked.

The woman shrugged slowly and lifted both brows. "Depends on who's asking. He's crazy as a loon, so I guess that makes him dangerous enough. Wouldn't want *my* daughter locked up with him."

Molly almost reeled. "Please. Where can we find him?"

"Take the main road out of town, follow it, oh, ten, twelve, fifteen miles? A good bit. Look for Hillbrook Farm, which is really a local honey stand now. Poor Dave Hillbrook got so sick, and his kids—he has six, you know—had to—"

"Where is Cutter's house?" Trace sliced into her story with enough urgency that the woman nodded in apology.

"Take a left after the stand onto a dirt road. Just follow it into the woods."

"And?"

"And…hope for the best."

Molly almost howled in agony at that, but Trace muttered a quick, "Thank you," and once again grabbed Molly's hand, this time to rush back to the Jeep. "When we get in the car, text everyone where we're going. Tell them to meet us there. Call the local sheriff. And please, God, tell me one of your brothers has a gun."

She just stared at him. "I'm going to pretend you didn't say that, man who spent fourteen years in prison for accidentally killing someone while defending someone else."

His jaw locked for a moment as he stared straight ahead. "And I'll spend the rest of my freaking life there to save my daughter and grandmother."

She honestly couldn't argue with that.

Despite the crowds, snowfall, and sense of impending doom, Trace drove as sanely as a man could. They narrowly missed another car changing lanes, fishtailed on some ice, and broke the speed limit more times than Molly could count, but they made it out of town. About seven miles away, she lost cell service, and that meant she was out of touch with her family, all of whom were somewhere behind them, making the same trek.

"There! There's a farm stand," Trace said, pointing to a battered sign on the side of the road.

"Does that say Hillbrook Farm?" Molly squinted through the falling snow. "Does it?" Then something red fluttered in the breeze. "What is that?"

They both stared at the splash of color hanging from a tree, the bright red completely out of place in the snow-covered woods.

"Is that…"

"It's the scarf I gave Pru last Christmas!" Molly actually screamed the announcement. "She's guiding us to her."

Trace threw her a look, silent, the expression in his dark eyes still a mix of terror and determination. "I hope so."

If not, then…no, Molly didn't want to think about what some local lunatic could do to her daughter and grandmother. No, she'd concentrate on the hope that scarf gave her. Holding that hope with everything she had, her head grew lighter. Her stomach queasy. And her heart felt like it might actually thump out of her chest.

Without a word, Trace took the next left a little too fast, revved the truck up a snow-covered hill, and rounded a corner. There, he slammed on the brakes at the sight of a maroon sedan half on the road, half in a ditch.

"Gramma's car!" Relief rushed over Molly so hard and fast, she couldn't breathe. Her hands were shaking as she yanked at the door handle and climbed out of the Jeep, noticing that Trace was even faster and out of the driver's seat first.

She slipped on snow and ice, but righted herself as she rushed to follow him to the car, stretching both arms to fill them with the two people she loved so much as he yanked open the front door.

Before she reached him, he whipped to the side and threw the back door open, too, but stood, silent and still, staring in.

She heard him mutter a curse, then forced herself to get next to him so she could see in the back. A blanket, wet, sticky, and covered in...

Oh, God.

Her head grew light, and suddenly darkness closed in around her.

"Trace..." She whispered his name as a wave of dizziness and nausea threatened. "Is that..."

But he was stumbling away, walking with his head down, then he fell to his knees and lifted some snow.

"There's a trail of... Oh my God, Molly, there's so much..."

Blood.

That was Molly's last thought before she crumpled to the ground.

Chapter Fourteen

Pru wasn't prepared for the Christmas cabin in the woods that Bill Cutter called home. It was literally the last place she'd ever expect this gruff Marine sniper to live. The A-shaped wooden structure was as heavy with colored lights as it was with snow, trimmed like the gingerbread house she helped her little cousin Christian make a few days ago. And through the front window, a fully decked-out Christmas tree glittered like Santa himself had decorated it.

So how dangerous could the mountain man actually be if he was that full of the holiday spirit? Strange, yes. Unexpected, definitely. But he wasn't going to kill...angels.

He used his shoulder to shove open the front door and marched inside without issuing an invitation to follow. But they did, and both Gramma and Pru had to stop and let their jaws drop open in surprise.

This room rivaled the Kilcannon living room for Christmas spirit, with lights everywhere and red ribbons, big bows, bells, garlands, and so many angels, and two stockings hanging from the mantel, where a few logs glowed from an earlier fire. And in the dining area, a life-size Nativity scene, complete with hand-carved Mary and Joseph statues and a couple of shepherds, took up almost the entire space.

Where the manger should be, a large whelping box crafted from a wood-slatted container rested, fully lined with plush blankets, pillows, and a well-chewed bunny rabbit slipper.

On the front of the box was a gold crown and the word *Queenie.*

Ooookay.

This man might look like a hardened criminal and live like a loony tune, but he obviously held a high regard for his dog and her litter, and the holiday. Didn't that tell Pru enough to feel safe?

She'd grown up around a lot of men who were mushballs when it came to dogs—maybe not quite this extreme, but what about her own father? Wasn't she the one who'd misjudged Trace Bancroft as a killer when the ex-con showed up at Waterford? But then she'd seen him nearly crack in half when he thought Meatball might die.

First impressions could be wrong…she hoped.

After Bill Cutter laid Blue in the box and adjusted the blankets around her, he straightened slowly, turning to let his bloodshot gaze shift from Gramma to Pru. "I'm Cutter. You saved Queenie."

His voice was thick, as if he fought tears, which explained the red-rimmed eyes in a way that made Pru's heart slide around in her chest.

"Not yet, we haven't," Pru said. "Her next pup is breech, and I think it's a big one. If it isn't turned, Blue, er, Queenie could bleed hard as it comes out."

As if to prove her point, Queenie whimpered and started panting louder, almost as if she'd gotten a second wind now that she was home.

"There, now." Gramma went to the whelping manger to gently settle the two new pups next to their momma. Pru leaned over and added the last one to the pack.

Gramma stroked them all, her old hand settling on the panting mama. "There we go, lass. You can do it, Blue."

"Her name's Queenie," Bill said under his breath. "And I'm Cutter."

"'Tis Blue to me," Gramma replied, lifting her chin and looking up a good foot at the man. "And we might need some professional help to have this last pup. You have a doctor on hand?"

He looked at her like she'd asked if he had a few Martians in the back room. The two of them just stared at each other until the silence went on a little bit too long.

"You save her," Cutter ordered. "You, little old angel."

Gramma snorted a soft laugh. "S'pose I've been called worse."

"Do you want me to, Gramma?" Pru asked, kneeling next to the box. "I can."

Very slowly, Gramma lifted a hand, still staring at their host. Or captor, depending on how you looked at the strange situation. "We'll do it together, Pru."

Suddenly, Cutter turned and grabbed a fluffy red and green pillow from the sofa and put it on the floor for Gramma to kneel on. She thanked him with a nod and held up her hands. "I need to wash up. And is it possible you have any latex gloves? What about a proper first aid kit? A bottle of lidocaine might actually save the day."

He blinked as if the requests had thrown him completely.

"I've been around farm animals my whole life, and my son and granddaughter are vets."

Another blink.

"The animal kind," Pru added, sensing that *vet* meant something else to this Marine.

"The dog needs a C-section," Gramma said. "And if we attempt that, she'll die. But if you don't want to call a professional, we'll try to turn the pup and hope for the best."

His only answer was a simple nod.

"Come on, Pru. Let's wash up." Without waiting for him to answer, she headed to the kitchen, which was partially visible through a doorway, and Pru followed.

There were even more Christmas decorations in there, including angel-themed hand towels that Pru used to dry off after thoroughly scrubbing her hands.

"Gramma, can you do this?" she asked in a hushed whisper. "'Cause there's no telling what this man will do if his Queenie dies."

"A woman can do what a woman has to do," she said.

"Old Irish proverb?"

"No, I saw it on Twitter." She shook her well-rinsed hands in the sink. "Let's do this."

"Oh, Gramma." Pru reached for her, careful not to touch her with sterilized hands, but so needing to hug this tiny creature who defied everyone and everything and every expectation. "I love you so much. I would be lost without you. You are the most amazing, wonderful woman I've ever known and…" She leaned back and smiled through tears. "I've known quite a few for someone only fourteen years old."

Gramma's eyes grew moist at the little speech. "Aye, Prudence Anne Kilcannon, so have I. And I wouldn't want anyone else next to me in times of good or bad."

They stared at each other for a long time, eye to eye, heart to heart, separated by more than seven decades, but as close as two women could be.

"And I really don't think he's going to kill us," Pru added. "Since we're angels and all."

"But you're right. There's no tellin' what he'll do if something happens to that dog."

Pru swallowed. "Then let's save her and her baby."

Together, they went back into the dining room-turned-Nativity set where Cutter was opening a large and extremely well-stocked first aid kit. Pru almost hooted in joy at the sight of packaged sterile surgical gloves, antibacterial ointment, and thick, clean gauze.

Gramma slipped on the gloves and knelt on the pillow Cutter had left for her. "The puppies aren't crying as much," she whispered.

"I stoked the fire." Cutter came to stand next to her and watch. "Will they eat?"

One worked its way toward its mama's belly to suckle a nipple, but Blue's focus seemed to be on the one that couldn't come out. "Soon," Gramma said. "Maybe after the last one's born."

"Why is she bleeding so much?" Cutter asked.

"I think she's torn some skin," Pru told him. "But

if you have any kind of cell service, I can have my mom here soon, and she could save the dog and the puppy."

He just stared at her. "I don't use phones."

"Internet?"

He shook his head.

"You have six thousand Christmas lights, but no phone and no computer?" The question came out laden with frustration, and Pru almost wished she hadn't said it, remembering that the groomer mentioned he suffered from agoraphobia. But he didn't seem angered by her question. In fact, his expression softened.

"Queenie likes Christmas," he said. "It's her favorite time of year. That's how I know you're angels."

Oh boy. No one at Waterford was even going to believe this when she told them.

Pru looked up at him. "Don't set the bar so high. We're just people."

He hesitated a moment, his time-worn complexion deepening in color. For a minute, Pru thought he was going to explode, but then his eyes welled up. "I prayed for angels to find Queenie and bring her home," he whispered. "And you came."

"Yes, we did," Gramma said, inching him away. "Now you have to let us concentrate and do the job. Tell me how she got lost if you want to talk, but sit over there, lad, on the sofa."

Lad? The guy was definitely in his seventies. But he followed the instructions and took a seat. "I don't like to talk," he muttered.

We noticed.

Pru leaned over the whelping box, and Gramma Finnie got settled and started working on Blue's breech pup. For a long time, she didn't say anything but cooed and coaxed Blue along.

Behind them, Cutter sighed in abject misery. "How long?"

"A little while," Pru said, her heart breaking for him. "Can I make you some tea?" she offered.

If the idea that one of his guests offered him something to drink seemed strange, ol' Bill Cutter didn't let on. "No." He leaned forward and put his head in his hands. "I just…can't live without her. I'd have no reason. No reason at all."

A little piece of Pru's heart broke as she settled on the floor next to the whelping box.

"Donchya be thinkin' about that, lad," Gramma said. "I can't turn it."

"You can't?" Pru and Cutter asked at the same time.

"I've fixed his feet, I think, so his legs won't be broken when he's born." She rested on her haunches, her gloved hands hanging in the box. "Now we just have to wait for Blue to be ready to give it a go."

"How long?" he asked again.

"It may be a while now," Gramma said vaguely. "She's very tired and we need to let her rest for the big finale. Try and think about other things until she's ready."

"There are no other things," he whispered sadly.

"How 'bout we sing you some Christmas carols?" Gramma suggested, adding her brightest smile.

He glared at her.

"A nice story?"

Pru bit her lip, almost laughing at Gramma's determination to calm the man down. Five more minutes and she'd be reciting 'Twas the Night Before Christmas, which was really pretty with her brogue.

"Finish the story you were telling me," Pru suggested. "It was Ireland in the 1940's."

Bill Cutter didn't even lift his head from his hands. That's how little interest he had in that idea.

"Aye, I could," Gramma said. "I had a beau that my father didn't like at all," she added, as if Bill Cutter actually cared.

At his silence, Gramma sighed, giving up too soon.

"Tell him, Gramma. Tell him about the pin we took to town and how you got it." Pru added a look she knew Gramma would understand. *This could be a while, and Cutter is losing it.*

She looked unsure, but slowly Gramma talked, giving a shorter, but no less colorful, recount of the sister who went off to be a nurse in the war, the boy who needed help, and how he'd found Finnie to return the pin.

Somewhere, during the story, Bill Cutter lifted his head. His eyes cleared, and he trained them on Finnie while she described running away from her farm to meet Seamus Kilcannon. When she stopped just short of that first kiss, he leaned forward.

"Don't tell me. He left and never showed again."

Gramma hooted softly. "What kind of a story would that be, lad?"

"A real one," he replied, his gruff voice thick with emotion and, Pru suspected, experience.

"Well, mine's real enough. It all happened in a place called Ballinaboola."

He choked a response. "Sounds like a fairy tale."

Gramma closed her eyes. "In some respects, it was. In others…a nightmare." She cleared her throat in a way that Pru recognized as the sound of Gramma Finnie about to tell a story.

Chapter Fifteen

Ballinaboola, Ireland 1949

Seamus was late.

Finnie pressed against the stone wall outside of the upholstery factory to ward off the cold, her empty stomach gnawing with hunger as she eyed the slate sky. There'd be more snow tonight, for sure. Fine. She could stick her poor swollen fingers in it and freeze off some of the pain.

She'd spent that day, like she'd spent six of them every week, turning stitches on pillows into words, each one meant to make the Irishman fortunate enough to lay his head on the cushion feel better.

Today, she'd stitched the same phrase twenty-two times.

There's nothing so bad it couldn't be worse.

She embroidered those words until her needle blister bled and the quittin' bell finally rang.

Well, yes, she thought as she stomped her thin leather boots against the creeping cold. Something could be worse than Seamus being late to meet her on a Saturday night. He could not show at all.

Of course, it was her greatest fear, but so far, it hadn't been realized. In fact, in the nearly three years since Seamus had come back from England, he'd never once shown any indication that there wouldn't be a next time. For months, it was only once a week, sometimes even fewer times than that. They'd meet when he was able to steal away from his family business and somehow get out to The Deeps, where they would walk, in rain, snow, or sun, away from everyone to their private world of Seamus and Finola.

They'd dream about a better life, a family of their own, a time without hunger and poverty. His father passed away, and Seamus took over the glassblowing business, and slowly, his fortunes began to change for the better. But the Brennan farm fell deeper into the rut that was common for rural Irish folk.

Then summer slipped into fall, and the harvest was slim that year. Come winter, Mammy's brother died of influenza, and they took in his wife and three children. Although her cousin Donal was another strapping lad to work the pastures, it still meant four more mouths to feed. When Finnie turned sixteen, Da came home and announced he'd found her a job in an upholstery factory in Ballinaboola.

She'd live in a parish house with a dozen other country girls, he told her, all working to help support their families.

Her family had all looked at her that day, expecting tears or a plea for a different plan, but Finnie had had to work hard to keep the smile off her face.

Ballinaboola was a stone's throw from the Kilcannon glassblowing business, and that meant...Seamus. All the time, any time she wasn't working.

She accepted her "fate" with grace that was applauded by Mammy and appreciated by Da. Edward called her a saint, and Patrick hugged her three extra times the day she left. Only Jack, her younger brother, who'd once caught Finnie and Seamus kissing under the alder tree, suspected she was not saintly at all. She'd spent the last year paying him off with all her biscuits, and that seemed to keep him quiet enough.

While the rest of Ireland battled a wretched winter and celebrated the fact that Ireland would soon be a republic, Finola Brennan perfected her stitching. With fingers as fast and nimble as any in the factory, she was soon moved to the specialty pillow department, where she and four other lassies were charged with memorizing Irish songs and proverbs in old books and turning them into cross-stitched pillows that sold at vendors all over the county.

It was grueling labor, but most evenings she could meet Seamus for half an hour, sometimes more. It was enough for the young couple to fall deeply, crazily, completely in love. She'd even met his family, and they liked her.

She'd never had the nerve to tell hers about him, though. When she was home, Da talked without end about one thing and one thing only—leaving the misery of Ireland and going to Amer—

"Finnie! Finnie! Hurry, lass. We must go!"

At the sound of a lad's voice and the clatter of cart wheels, she whipped around, ready to see the handsome face of the one she loved, but she sucked in a shocked breath at the sight of her eldest brother, Patrick.

"What are you doing here?" Panic made her voice rise. Seamus couldn't be far away now, maybe around any corner. What would—

"In the cart, lass." He brought Alphonsus to a stop and reached his hand down, closing his fingers around her wrist to yank. "No time to waste."

"I can't leave now. I can't—"

"Yer leavin' now and yer leavin' forever." Strong as an ox, Patrick easily lifted her off the ground, her feet dangling for one wild second before he planted her next to him. "Da got passage, Finnie! For all of us. He's waiting at the port, and we leave in an hour for America!"

"America?" She choked the word. She couldn't go to America!

"Mam's at the parish right now collecting your stuff. I just got your last pay." He grinned as if she should welcome this intrusion into her life. "Off we go!" He gave a good flip of the reins to Alphonsus. "We're giving the horse to Aunt Bridget, and she's taking over the farm. Donal can run it well enough."

Finnie put both hands on her head as if that could stop its spinnin'. "We're leaving the farm? Leaving County Wexford?" It couldn't be. It *couldn't.*

Patrick let out a hearty laugh and easily guided the horse back onto the road, the big wooden cart wheels rocking over the mud and ruts. "We're going to America, Finola. A whole new world and a whole new life. You should be celebrating, Sister, not looking back."

But she was looking back, her whole body turned to peer past another horse and a group of men to the corner that Seamus should be turning any minute.

And there he was, right where she'd been one minute ago, staring at her with the same look she had to be wearing on her face. Shock. Horror. Disbelief. And the sickening sensation that they were losing everything.

"Seamus." She mouthed his name.

He just stared, hands in his pockets, confusion on his face.

She pressed her fingers to her mouth to keep from screaming out. Would Patrick help her? Would he let her stay?

Not a chance. He was firmly in Da's lane on every decision the family made. The eldest Brennan would never go against their father, the very man he was named after.

"Seamus," she whispered. His figure became smaller as distance, noise, horses, and people separated them. She lowered her hands and tried to get the message to him. "America," she said, knowing he couldn't possibly hear her. "America."

Had he heard? Would he know where to go?

"America!" She screamed it at the top of her lungs, making Patrick throw an arm around her in a rare display of affection and good humor.

"'Tis right, Finnie. We are going to a place called Ellis Island, and everything will change. Everything."

As she lost sight of Seamus, Finnie finally turned in her seat. "Everything." Her whisper caught on the sob in her throat. How would he ever find her? How could she live without him?

"There's Mammy and Edward." Patrick pointed across the slushy street where her mother stood next to her brother, each holding a bundle of clothes and her bedding. "Go help," he said, giving her a nudge out of the cart. "And move quick, Finnie! That ship won't wait for us!"

Maybe they could miss it. Maybe she could delay this nightmare. Fall and twist her ankle or faint dead away—either was likely, considering how dizzy she was as she narrowly missed a wagon full of chickens.

"Did ya hear, lass?" her mother called, lifting her pile of wool like it was absolute proof of the news. "'Tis happening! 'Tis truly happening."

Finnie slowed her step and pressed a hand to her heart. When was the last time she'd seen her mother's smile? When was the last time Mary Margaret Brennan let out a trill of a laugh that sounded just like...just like Vi's?

That was the last time. The night before Vi broke every heart in their family and went to war. Six months later, a letter came...and Mammy hadn't smiled, laughed, or even walked with a straight back since.

Vi's death had crushed her, and America gave her hope. A future. A plan for security, if not prosperity.

She reached her mother, who actually tried to hug her with her armload of stuff. "I don't need help, lass. Get the sheets and blankets from Edward, and we'll wrap it all up in the cart. We must hurry. The ship leaves in an hour."

Finnie blinked at her. "Do I have to go?"

Mammy's smile disappeared instantly. "Did I hear you right, Finola?"

There it was again. All the hurt, all the grief, all the loss that Vi caused darkened her mother's aging features. Could Finnie do the same thing to this poor woman? What kind of daughter would that make her?

"I mean...do I go without checking my bed and drawer?" she said quickly. "Did you get everything?"

"Aye, all that matters." She dipped her head. "Including that pin. I know what it means to ya."

Her heart tripped. Mammy didn't really know what it meant. She thought it was a memory of Vi, and Da had removed nearly every reminder of the eldest Brennan from the farm, so as to protect his heart. But Mammy let Finnie keep the broken pin, maybe not even knowing it had been returned by Seamus.

Her father had never mentioned the visit from the lad who had brought something for Finnie.

"What are you standin' there for?" Patrick called as he rounded the group with Alphonsus kicking up filthy, melting snow. "Climb in and let's go, Brennans! We're off to America!"

Mammy's joy returned, and Edward started singing, and Patrick helped them all in with ease and efficiency. In a matter of minutes, Ballinaboola was far behind them.

Along with Seamus, the man Finnie loved and meant to marry.

With a shaky breath, she looked up at her mother. "Mammy," she whispered.

"Not now, Finnie." Her mother leaned closer to Patrick. "Watch that turn ahead, lad. The road's washed out up here. The last thing we need is a delay."

Patrick just laughed, his confidence at an all-time

high. "Donchya be worryin', Mam. I'll get us there. I'll get us to America."

"Please, Mammy. I need—"

"Here you go." Her mother reached into her pocket and pulled out a familiar lace kerchief, wrapped tight around her most treasured belonging. "I wouldn't lie to you, lass. You hold it for luck now. We're going to need it."

Luck that somehow, someday, somewhere, Seamus Kilcannon would find her yet again.

Edward kept singing like a loon, and Mammy inched closer to Patrick as if that could help him get them there faster, while Finnie just sank deeper into the seat and strangling ache for her loss. All she could do was run her finger over the horseshoe at the center of the pin.

They never even said goodbye.

She closed her eyes and tried to imagine how impossible that would have been anyway. When she finally opened them, they were right at Wexford Port, the very place where she'd first met Seamus Kilcannon.

She turned to see the docks, which hadn't changed, and realized that Patrick was going to leave the cart and horse at the same stone wall where she had parked it the day she'd brought Vi here. How was that for the fates laughing at her? What were the chances?

Dismal. Just like her chances of ever seeing Seamus again.

She was rushed out of the cart, stumbling along to keep up with her family, clinging to her meager belongings wrapped in a blanket. A light snow started to fall, but nothing could dampen the spirits of her family.

In minutes, they found Da and Jack and Aunt Bridget and her wee Colleen, along with cousins Maura and Donal. There were hugs and kisses and promises and goodbyes.

All things she had been denied with Seamus.

"Don't let me see that long face, lass." Aunt Bridget chucked Finnie's chin playfully. "We'll be coming over in a year or two, and by then ye'll be married to a fine American boy."

They all guffawed at that like it was…funny. Or possible.

"I won't marry, Aunt Bridget." Somehow, it felt like saying it made it true. She'd never marry anyone but Seamus Kilcannon.

But her comment was lost in the commotion of the many families rushing to get on board and get into some rat-filled underdeck that would be home for the days and weeks of the crossing.

Didn't matter. Finnie would just sit in a corner and cry.

Once again, she was hustled through the crowds, jostled against strangers, forced to give her name to someone, and pressed into the pack of Brennans as they moved like cattle to slaughter.

Da led the way, his head held high, his victory clear. He was saving his family, getting them out of the dregs of poverty and famine, leaving behind his homeland for a new world.

A world without Seamus, which was no world at all.

Finally, they were at the top of the ramp, their feet on the swaying deck of a ship that Finnie could barely see through her tears.

"Bid farewell," Mammy whispered to her as she eyed the docks from a completely different angle.

The boys called out to no one and everyone, and Da made the sign of the cross. But Finnie merely stood in shock at how her world had turned upside down and inside out in the space of an hour. Tears spilled down her cheeks.

"Oh, lass. Someday you can come back, if you ever get tired of America."

"I don't want to leave, Mammy," she managed to say, giving in to a sob. "Not now, not ever."

"Aye, and you'll change your mind." She grabbed Finnie's hand and gripped hard. "It's a new start, Daughter. A new life. A chance to stop livin' starved and poor."

Finnie looked directly into her mother's eyes, as blue as her own, praying that Mary Margaret Brennan had once felt this way about Da. It seemed inconceivable, but if she had, Mammy might understand.

"I love someone, Mam."

She blinked at her as if she most certainly did *not* understand.

"You…what?"

"I'm in love."

"Look at that lad," Patrick said, grabbing her arm and pointing back to the docks. "He's lost his mind."

They all turned, but it was Finnie who gasped as the rest laughed.

She stared at the figure down on the wooden boards, along with nearly every eye on the ship. How could you not look as Seamus Kilcannon jumped up and down, waved his hands and cap, then shook off his coat and waved that, too.

"Seamus." Finnie's heart somehow managed to stay in her chest. Somehow. But it might not be there long, not the way it was hammerin' right then.

Of course, everyone *had* to look at him.

Everyone...including Finnie. And wasn't that exactly what he wanted?

Yes, he was forcing her to find him, since he couldn't find her.

"Seamus," she said again, louder.

Mammy squeezed her hand, and she felt Da's gaze level on her, but she couldn't wipe the smile from her face or the soaring, fluttering wings of joy in her chest.

"Finola!" Even over the clanging of the masts, the great groans of the ship, and hundreds of people, she swore she could hear her name on his lips. "Finola Brennan! Don't leave me!"

He'd made such a spectacle that many of those people were hushed, and she really could hear him.

And so could Da.

Next to her, she felt her father bristle. And her mother's hand loosen its grip ever so slightly.

"He's calling Finnie," Edward muttered in disbelief.

"You know that lad?" Patrick asked.

Jack just looked hard at her, since he knew the answer to that question.

"Finola Brennan!" Seamus's loud voice floated up to the deck. His gaze scanned from one side to the other, still unable to find her, but that didn't stop him from calling out.

Yes, she was meant to find him. And now she had...so what should she do?

"Is that the one?" Mammy asked under her breath.

Finnie nodded. "Aye."

"Marry me, Finola Brennan! Get off that ship and marry me!"

Finnie pressed her hands to her chest. She'd long ago dropped the blanket bundle but still held tight to that pin…the very piece of metal that had brought him back to her. The horseshoe and shamrock and broken metal dug into her skin.

All around, a hum of interest and talk started as more and more people stopped their conversations to take in the drama. Everyone had a thought, a chuckle, a word of wisdom.

Everyone but Da, whose stare was so unwavering that Finnie felt like her cheek would melt under the fire of his glare.

Finally, Finnie took her gaze off of Seamus to meet her father's.

"Don't even think about it, Finola Brennan."

She exhaled. "Please, Da. Please."

Silent, he sliced her with a challenge and a dare in his eyes. And there was pain, too. Deep pain. He'd already lost one daughter, but his damn pride could cost him another.

Mammy's fingers loosened some more. Her touch turned from a panicked grasp to something softer and more tender. Finnie turned to find out where Mammy stood.

Her eyes said it all. But she added words, too. "If he really loves you…"

"He does," she said softly.

"Then…"

Finnie spun back to her father, desperate for the right answer, for permission, for love.

"If you get off this ship and go to him," he ground out, "you're as dead to me as Vi."

"Da." Her voice cracked.

"Finola! I see you!" Seamus started leaping again, wild with his discovery. "Don't leave! Marry me. I love you, Finola Brennan! I love you!"

"What should I do?" she cried.

No one answered as Finnie stood, precariously balanced between the past and the future, pulled by love in two different directions.

"Oh Lord. What should I do?"

Chapter Sixteen

"What should I do?"

Neither Cutter nor Gramma Finnie heard Pru's plea for help, as they were both staring at each other, enraptured by the story. Which was a good one, no doubt about it, but...

"It's time," Pru said. "But the pup is coming out backward, and it's stuck."

Cutter leaped closer. "What do you mean, stuck?"

Gramma had already settled on the cushion, lost in her own story, while Pru had listened but kept an eye on the pup. But now, Gramma pushed up and leaned into the whelping box, putting her hands on Blue.

"It'll come through," Gramma assured them. "Blue just has to be strong."

But Pru just shook head. She'd already watched the struggle. "This one's big. Way too big. Blue—er, Queenie has had enough. And I hate to tell you this, but she's really losing blood now."

Cutter paled as if he were the one losing blood, falling to his knees next to the whelping box. "Come on, girl," he muttered. "Get this last one out. These angels can fix you up."

Pru looked up at Gramma Finnie and gave a little shake of her head to communicate just how dire this situation was. Gnawing on her lower lip and studying the bloody mess inside, Gramma got the message, Pru could tell.

"'Tis quite a bit of blood," she murmured. "But I've seen worse."

Cutter leaned in as if he might try to pick up his dog and squeeze the puppy out, but Gramma stopped him with one bloody latex-covered hand. "Let me help her."

"I don't care about the pup." He wiped his eyes and blinked into the box again, falling to his knees to join them as they knelt at the homemade manger. "Just save Queenie. Please, oh, please save her."

"I'm going to try and save both," Gramma said. "You two just stay back."

She leaned into the box and worked her hand into the birth canal, closing her eyes, breathing as heavily as the pup.

"He's fully backward," she reported. "No chance of turnin'. Legs up."

Cutter actually moaned.

"He'll come soon enough," she promised. But Pru knew that Queenie's poor body would take a beating.

Muttering what Pru suspected was an old Irish prayer, Gramma focused every ounce of concentration on the dogs. Sweat dampened the gray hairs at her temples, and her little body trembled as she worked the pup out. Precious minutes ticked. Blood oozed. And poor Queenie seemed to drift in and out of consciousness.

"Come on now, big boy. Help your mama out." With gentle words and a strong hand, she urged him out until finally the pup's backside appeared.

And Queenie whimpered in pain.

A fresh gush of blood poured from her torn flesh, but that must have been nature's way of helping things along. The additional space was all the puppy needed to plop out, sliding onto the pillows butt first.

Queenie didn't turn or lick or even move. She just stared straight ahead with sheer agony in her eyes.

Then she closed them.

"No!" Cutter cried, lunging for the box. "She can't die!"

He reached in to hold her as Gramma eased the new pup out of the way. Cutter sobbed silently, while Gramma and Pru stroked the transparent sac to free the baby. He squirmed, eyes closed.

"We're losing her." Cutter's voice was ragged and wrecked. "She's going to die. She's going to die!"

A loud noise shook the whole house as the front door thudded open. "She better not die!"

They all turned in shock to see Trace marching in with his fists clenched and arms up. Yes, he'd accidentally killed a man with those fists, and Pru was quite certain he was prepared to do that again.

"No, stop!" Pru yelled.

Right behind him, Mom rushed into the house, her tear-stained face telling the whole story.

"Mom, please!" Pru was up in a second, putting her body between Cutter and the two people who loved her most. "You have to save this dog!"

"Pru!" She threw her arms around Pru, practically suffocating her. "Oh my God, you're alive."

"But she might not be." Pru whipped around to point at the whelping box.

Gramma was holding her bloody gloves in the air. "Don't hurt him, lad. Donchya be throwin' punches. We're trying to keep a dog alive."

Pru forced her mother to look at Queenie. "All that blood, Mom. The last one was turned and born backward. We don't know how to help her."

"I do." Mom swallowed and took a deep breath, instantly falling to her knees in the spot where Pru had been. "In the back of the Jeep, Garrett keeps a canine first aid kit. Get it, fast. And pack some snow in a bowl. A lot of it. I need a needle and thread, as sterile as possible. Go. *Now.* We have only seconds to spare."

Molly shifted into vet mode the minute she put her hands on the dog. She barely glanced at the gray-haired, bearded man she nudged to the side, aware that he was sobbing and reluctant to let go.

All she knew was he had not hurt Pru or Gramma and this collie was, indeed, critical. She should have had a C-section, no doubt, but now Molly had to stop the bleeding and sew up the episiotomy that nature had given her. And pray there was no lasting internal damage.

She heard Trace and Pru go outside and took the pair of clean gloves Gramma handed to her. "Take the puppies," Molly instructed. "Get them wrapped in blankets by the fire. Keep them warm."

"You heard her," Gramma said, giving the old man a decent push. "You take two, and I'll take two—"

"But Queenie is dying."

"Not in my granddaughter's hands."

He still didn't move, and Gramma got up on her tiptoes, reaching about the middle of his chest, which she poked. "You do what the angels say."

That worked. He instantly unfroze and grabbed some clean towels that were piled up on the side of... Molly lifted her head and took in her surroundings. She was in a life-size replica of a stable, with a wooden Mary and Joseph staring down at her, backed up by a four-foot-tall shepherd.

How the heck had they ended up here?

It didn't matter. Gramma and Pru were safe. Right now, the only thing that mattered was this dog who'd had a traumatic tear from a big breech pup and wasn't healthy enough to fight back.

The sounds of their conversation and the insane amount of Christmas lights faded into the background as Molly mopped blood and found the source. When Trace handed her the opened first aid kit, he settled to her right, and Pru took her left.

They worked as quietly and efficiently as her vet techs, but then, both Pru and Trace had stood next to her during surgery before. Pru threaded the needle. Trace helped her clean and freeze the wound with snow that turned red and soaked the blankets. And poor Queenie continued to fall in and out of awareness.

When Molly inserted the needle to make the first stitch, the dog startled, and her eyes opened wide for the first time. Even shadowed with pain and surprise, the one blue eye and one golden-brown eye made for a haunting image.

"Pretty, huh?" Pru whispered as if she'd read Molly's thoughts.

"Mmm." She was concentrating too hard to talk. Plus, when she did talk to Pru, it wasn't going to be idle chatter about a dog's eyes.

"Gramma said that dogs with two different-colored eyes go to heaven twice. Once when they're alive, but then they come back. And again, when they die."

"Then let's hope this is the first time," Molly said, shoving the needle into thick flesh and nodding for Trace to pack ice over that while she pulled the thread.

"I know you're really mad at me," Pru whispered.

"Beyond," Molly acknowledged.

"You, too?" Pru asked Trace.

He answered with a long, slow sigh. "Not as much as your mom is. Honest, I'm proud of you."

"Proud?" Pru and Molly asked the question in perfect unison, which would have been funny, except *nothing* was right now.

"Yes. Proud."

Molly angled her head, breaking her concentration on the stitches long enough to shoot Trace a look of disbelief.

"Look what she did, babe," he explained, gesturing to the dog and puppies. "She could have run, left the dog, chickened out. But she put the animal first, which is exactly what her mother would have done."

Against her will, Molly felt her heart soften. A little. "She also scared her mother to death."

"Well, I'm proud of her for handling a tough situation. Proud of you, Umproo. Proud of my daughter."

Next to her, Molly could feel Pru's sigh of relief. "Thanks." She leaned in a little closer to look past Molly to Trace. "Dad."

Molly bit her lip, fighting both tears and laughter. "Really pulling out all the stops, Pru."

Trace laughed a little, too, reaching his arm around Molly's back. Behind her, she could feel Trace and Pru squeeze each other's hands, making a chain of support around her.

She nearly collapsed with love for both of them that hit as strong as that wave of dizziness had, only this time it was from relief and joy and maybe a little stress as the dog under her hands moaned.

Biting her lip, she continued the stitches, one after another, as tight as she could make them, each one stemming more of the flow of blood. Finally, the wound was closed, and the worst of the pain was over for poor Queenie.

As if she sensed that, the dog slumped onto clean towels, whimpered, and fell asleep.

"Will she live?" The question came from behind Molly and startled her. Trace and Pru broke their linked hands so Molly could turn and look up at the mountain man who had most certainly seen better days. He held two puppies, one in each arm, cradled and swathed in blankets.

"I think so," Molly said as gently as she could, pushing up to a stand. Trace and Pru did the same, flanking her protectively. "I think she's strong and wants to live for those pups."

His eyes welled with tears, and he tried to talk, but his face grew a little redder with each word, which Molly took for real, deep shyness.

"You're angels," he rasped. "Every one of you. A heavenly host of angels who came to save my Queenie."

Molly smiled. "We're just a dog-loving family," she told him. "And you need to give her time and love. She's going to be okay." Then she turned to Pru, raising one eyebrow as a reminder that not everyone was going to get out of this escapade entirely unscathed.

"Mom, I'm really sorry." She fisted her hands and pressed her knuckles to her mouth. "Don't kill me, please. It was—"

"My fault." Gramma stood from her chair next to a roaring fire, taking a step away from the bundled towels where the two other puppies were being warmed. "Pru was trying to make my life better. And I got a little carried away with the adventure. And..." She shifted her gaze to the whelping box. "Blue."

"Queenie," Cutter corrected.

Molly sighed and looked at Pru. "You know better."

"Mom, I wanted the somethings to be amazing because—"

"You feel cut off from the wedding because of Cassie."

Pru swallowed guiltily. "It all seems ridiculous now," she said. "I am so sorry I upset you. Were you really mad?"

"Still am," she said. "And mad that I fainted at the sight of blood on snow."

"You fainted?" Pru gasped and reached for her. "Oh God, Mommy. I'm so sorry."

The use of the old childhood *Mommy* and the

genuine agony in Pru's expression melted Molly's heart like the snow they'd used to numb Queenie's pain. Closing her eyes, she embraced Pru, and they both hugged for a long, precious moment.

"I'm sorry, too, child." Gramma added to the hug, and then they all inched back to see Trace beaming at them.

"Nothing quite like Kilcannon women loving each other."

"Kilcannon!" Cutter exclaimed, turning to Gramma. "Then you—"

Just then, the room was filled with the sound of truck engines and tires crunching snow, flashing red lights, and then some loud and familiar voices.

"And speaking of Kilcannons," Trace said, pointing at the window. "I believe at least a dozen more of them just arrived."

"*You got off the boat?*" Cutter practically flattened Gramma with the strength of the question.

"Of course I got off the boat, lad!" She gave a typical Gramma Finnie giggle. "It appears I've always had a bit of a reckless streak, and I guess that's how we ended up here, with me tryin' to recapture my youth." With a sigh, she shook her old white head and pinned her gaze on Pru. "For everything, there is a season. And I think we both, Pru and I, learned to embrace the season of life where we are, nine or ninety, and enjoy it for what it is."

Cutter stepped closer, bearing down on Gramma. "Wait. Finish the story. You got off the boat and..." He held out his hands in question.

"And we married, moved to America, made up with my family, and started one of our own, which has grown quite large and is, if I'm not mistaken, currently gathering in your yard."

"Have you ever thought about writing this down?" he asked.

Gramma hooted. "If you'd join this century, lad, and get a little somethin' called Wi-Fi up here, you could read my blog. And come to think of it, I *shall* tell that whole story. Spread it out over plenty of posts. Aye, my readers would love that." She beamed at him as they walked toward the door that Trace had already gone out. "'Tis a fine idea. I believe you've cracked my writer's block. Now, go outside and meet your guests because I'd venture the clan will be spendin' Christmas Eve right here. Have you a lantern I could put in the window? It's Irish tradition."

Molly turned to Pru, who was biting her lip and fighting tears, barely paying attention to anything but the movement, people, and lights outside.

"They all came after us." Her voice cracked. "The whole family."

Molly nodded. "I'm guessing the Mahoneys, too, who probably rounded up the local fire department. And Aidan and Beck flew here, and are no doubt out there, too."

"On Christmas Eve!" she practically wailed. "Oh God, I'm the worst."

Molly searched her face, lost for a moment in eyes the same color as her own, but so young and sweet and unlike any other human who'd ever walked the earth.

"You are not the worst, Pru," Molly whispered, bringing her closer for another hug. "You're safe and alive, and I guess when I get over how upset I was, I will realize that I should have been more in tune with what was bothering you. And like Trace—"

"You mean Dad," Pru interjected.

Molly smiled. "Like *Dad*, I'm proud that you risked your safety to save a dog and make Gramma happy again."

Outside, they could hear men's voices and a few women's, all rising with concern as they fired off questions that Trace had gone to field.

At the sound, Pru pressed her face into Molly's shoulder. "I am so sorry."

Molly stroked Pru's hair with nothing but love and forgiveness. "Baby, we all make bad decisions. My mother used to tell me we are not the sum total of our mistakes." Of course, she'd said that the day Molly admitted that she'd had a one-night stand in a minivan and Pru was the result.

Pru leaned back. "But you fainted, Mom."

"I know. I haven't even ever been dizzy like that in my life except...except..." That week before she made the confession to her mother. "Once before."

Pru's eyes flashed, instantly following Molly's thoughts, as she so often did. "Mom!"

"Pru..."

"It worked!" Pru exclaimed.

"Something did," Molly joked as the realization hit her heart and sent her reeling.

"Exactly," Pru said. "It's the 'somethings' surprise." Pru leaned closer. "'Shock the bride with old, new, borrowed, and blue, and she'll be favored with not one child but two.' That's the old Irish proverb Gramma quoted."

"I think she made that up, honey." *Didn't she?*

"Oh no, she didn't. Gramma worked in an upholstery factory and memorized all those Irish poems and things she says. Did you know that? And...and...Mom!" Pru's sadness evaporated as her pretty face lit up as bright as the tree behind her. "You're pregnant!"

Suddenly, Gramma Finnie had both her arms around them, beaming. "How could you think I made that up?"

"I'm..." Molly choked softly. "Is it possible?"

Pru squeezed her. "Yes, and now you have something new."

"And the pin I just retrieved from the jewelry store in town is something old."

"I have an idea." Gramma pointed to the whelping box where Queenie had lifted her head and looked around, no doubt searching for her puppies. Just that much movement assured Molly that the dog would survive her difficult labor. "Pru and I can borrow Blue, and we'll have those two covered, too. Would Cassie like that?"

Molly angled her head at Pru. "More important, do *you* like that?"

"I love it. And you. And my new baby sibling!" More tears sprang, but this time they were from pure joy. "Merry Christmas to us!"

Molly just put her head back and laughed while Pru and Gramma did a little dance around the Nativity scene, making Blue bark and bark at the angels who'd saved her.

You are cordially invited to attend the wedding of Molly Kilcannon and Trace Bancroft…it's free and available to my newsletter subscribers! Sign up at www.roxannestclaire.com/newsletter-2/ and download the festivities!

And once you're a newsletter subscriber, you'll be alerted when I have a new release, including Dogfather book nine—***Old Dog New Tricks***. Yes, readers, it's time for the Dogfather himself to find love.

Readers can join the private Facebook group of
Dogfather fans for inside scoop, secret tidbits,
and fun giveaways!
www.facebook.com/groups/roxannestclairereaders/

Or follow me on social media for fun, games, dogs,
and more!
www.facebook.com/roxannestclaire
www.twitter.com/roxannestclaire
www.instagram.com/roxannestclaire1

Turn the page for a Christmas surprise! Last year's holiday novella, ***Santa Paws is Coming to Town,*** has never been in print before due to its shorter length. Because so many readers who prefer a physical book have asked me for it, I've included the story here. Consider it one more flashback, and another Christmas with the Kilcannons!

Santa Paws Is Coming to Town

Copyright © 2017 Roxanne St. Claire

Chapter One

D aniel Kilcannon descended the stairs as a snowy late afternoon slipped into deep winter darkness. He took a moment to peek into the formal living room. The parlor, as it had been called when he was a child growing up on Waterford Farm, was rarely used now. But in December, that changed. Every square inch was festooned with gold and red and way too many twinkling white lights. They filled one corner with a nine-foot tree weighed down with a lifetime of collected ornaments, topped by a cherub they called Johnny Angel, who sported battery-powered wings that fluttered incessantly all season long.

Daniel tried to stand back and drink it all in, but the only thing he wanted to drink was a straight shot of Jameson's.

At his feet, Rusty gave a low grumble, as if he was not a fan of the hollow holiday, either.

"Hush, boy," he mumbled to his setter. "It's our secret."

He would never let his Christmas-loving clan know that of the very few things he hated in this world, the holidays topped the list. At least they had since Annie died.

Forcing himself into the room he'd avoided for the past few weeks as his daughters, granddaughter, and mother gleefully overdecorated, he went to the fireplace to add a log and stoke the dying flames back to life.

Rusty padded next to him and nuzzled his nose against Daniel's leg, always in tune with his master's emotions. Daniel absently rubbed the dog's head in a silent apology for having the blues on Christmas Eve.

He took a few steps closer to the tree, a sturdy and thick fir his sons had cut from the north end of Waterford Farm. Getting the tree from their own land was another tradition that hadn't died with Annie.

The fact was, his family seemed to be taking great pains to make Christmas like it had always been, and Daniel had no desire to stop them. Three of his sons were married or about to be. One had a stepchild now and a new baby on the way. His grief shouldn't stop this family from making new memories.

Speaking of memories, this tree had so many hanging on it, he could barely home in on just one. Some ornaments dated back forty years, like the glass globe engraved with "Baby from Heaven in '77" that his mother had given Annie when she was expecting Liam. And there was a cute little dog house with six doors, each with a different hand-painted name under a sign that read "The Kilcannon Kids 1990."

Next to that hung a small porcelain frame with a close-up of Annie and Daniel on their wedding day. He touched the filigreed edge, his gaze locked on his beautiful wife's face. So young, so scared, so damn perfect.

"Oh, Annie girl. How I miss you."

Rusty huffed out a dog sigh and settled on the floor, staring at the glittering gift wrap, no doubt picturing the upcoming mayhem that always ended with the boys making paper balls and the dogs going crazy trying to play catch in the house.

Then, Daniel would work to cover his sadness, but only so his family could have joy, laughter, teasing, the annual stupid T-shirts from Shane, and tears from Darcy when she got overwhelmed with emotion. He'd roll his eyes with them as Gramma presented her Irish proverbs on cross-stitch pillows and laugh when his sons teased each other about their abysmal wrapping skills.

Well, not all his sons. No Aidan at home this year. His youngest son was in Afghanistan, he now knew, after months of a more secretive assignment in the military. Hopefully, Aidan was having some sort of Christmas cheer courtesy of the US Army. He sighed as disappointment battled with grief and erased any chance of peace, joy, or much goodwill toward men in Daniel's heart.

"It's nothing short of sinful to be sad on Christmas Eve, lad."

He turned at the sound of his mother's voice. She stood in the entryway holding up a metal lantern darn near half the size of her tiny frame.

"I'm not sad."

She gave a look that reminded him that Finnie Kilcannon had known him for every minute of his sixty years and certainly knew when he was lying.

"Look at this." She shimmied the lantern back and forth to show off the unlit candle inside. "Found it at the antiques fair last summer, and I've been savin' it for this very night. Isn't she a beauty? Best we've ever had."

"If you want the Bitter Bark Fire Department to stop by." He took the glass and metal contraption from her hands and angled his head toward the picture window. "The usual place?"

"The biggest window in the house, that's what the Irish tradition commands," she said, nudging him that way. "And yes, we want the fire department, and friends, family, neighbors, and a priest, if he happens by. That's the whole reason of the Christmas candle, as you know."

"Oh, I know." He'd heard his mother recite the Irish folklore surrounding the placement of the candle for all of his Christmas Eves, and he would again tonight. "Should we light it now?"

She drew her brows together, adding to the many lines on her eighty-six-year-old parchment-soft face. "And deny me the chance to bore my entire family with the annual story of why we light it?"

He laughed softly. "Why wreck tradition now?"

"Speaking of tradition." She adjusted her bright red and white Christmas cardigan and leaned a little closer. "'Tis this time that Seamus and I would break out a wee bit of Jameson's. What do you say that we have one for old times?"

"I say I was just thinking that." He went to the bar they'd already set up in the kitchen and took two of the family shot glasses. The Waterford crystal was heavy, a reminder that the company that made it had been the source of his father's small fortune, and the reason Seamus Kilcannon could move his wife and

178

son to America. Of course, they'd named this land in the foothills of the Blue Ridge Mountains Waterford Farm as a nod to the glass empire that had helped build another. No glass blowing here, though. Just a lot of dogs.

"But it's hardly like old times, Gramma." He'd long ago given up calling her Mom. This little woman was Gramma Finnie to his children, the townsfolk, and the ever-growing audience of blog followers that she attracted with her whimsical musings online.

She settled in at the counter, her petite red velvet shoes dangling from under a black skirt. "Because our better halves are gone?" she asked.

Straight to the quick, that's where his mother cut, usually followed by one of her favorite sayings from the old country.

"Those who leave us don't go away," she said with a lilting Irish accent. "They walk beside us every day."

Smiling with a burst of love for this rock of dependability, he poured shots and brought one to her.

"*Sláinte.*" They said it in unison, but neither drank. Instead, his mother stared at him from behind her bifocals, then she lowered them as if she couldn't quite believe what she was seeing.

"What?" he asked.

"Oh, you just sounded so much like Seamus when you said that."

"'Cause there was nothing my father liked more than a shot of whiskey."

"There you'd be wrong, child. He loved you and Colleen and…" Her gaze drifted away, to the candle. "You know."

He knew. His uncle Liam, who died as a child. "This is not a good night to wallow in the children who aren't here."

"Amen to that." She took a deep drink, then asked, "Any word from Afghanistan?"

He shook his head. "'Peacekeeping' missions are harder than they sound, but Aidan is fine."

"Of course he is. Your youngest son is an invincible warrior."

God, he hoped so. "He'll call tomorrow, I'm sure, and that'll be the best Christmas present I'll get."

"Enough for you to let go of that bag of sorrow you're cartin' around like Santa's pack?"

He drew back. "I am not."

"I see through ya, laddie."

"Well, you're my mother."

She grinned, pounded back the Jameson's, and put the glass down hard on the granite. "Aye, I am, and happy to be." She leaned forward and air-kissed his cheek. "Don't worry, no one can tell but me. You're doing this family a favor by keeping the traditions alive even though the real keeper of the flame left us far too soon."

Everyone knew Annie Kilcannon was a Christmas fanatic.

He finished the dregs of his shot and pushed the glass aside, not wanting another, grateful for the sight of headlights in the driveway. "Looks like Colleen and the kids are here."

Daniel rose to greet his sister and her family, none of whom were technically "kids" anymore. Opening the kitchen door, since they'd never come to the front, he braced for a blast of cold North Carolina air and a warm hug from every one of the Mahoneys he loved so dearly.

Colleen and her youngest, Ella, came in first, shivering and laden with gifts.

"Hey, Uncle Daniel." Ella breezed in, aimed an air kiss his way and moved on. "Is Darcy upstairs?" Of course, Ella wouldn't spend a minute in this house without her beloved cousin. The two of them had been glued at the hip since they were born days apart thirty years earlier.

"She's over at her workroom, grooming a dog," Daniel said.

"She's working on Christmas Eve?" Colleen asked, brushing back a lock of thick dark hair that escaped the same waist-long braid she'd worn since high school. The only person who hated change more than Daniel was his younger sister, even though a better hairstyle would have probably suited her attractive features and fifty-four years.

"We got a new rescue in today, and oh, that poor thing was a hot mess," Daniel replied. "A little terrier that's skittish as heck, definitely abused and abandoned."

"Oh!" Ella put her hands over her mouth, drawing her brows in a frown. "How can you bear it?"

"We bear it because not only did Darcy give him the perfect name of Jack Frost, we've already found him a loving home."

"You have?" That question came from Braden, the middle Mahoney and the quietest of Colleen's crew. At thirty-three, he was as strapping as his older brothers, Declan and Connor, and as good-looking as Daniel's own sons, but Braden was never the center of attention.

Daniel greeted all three young men with hugs and pats on their strong backs. "Remember a few weeks ago when Chloe organized the Santa Paws Pet Adoption in Bushrod Square?" he asked.

"Oh yes," Colleen said. "I darn near came away with *another* Saint Bernard."

"Well, there was a little girl with her heart set on a Jack Russell, but someone else got it," Daniel said. "Then we got a call this afternoon from the fire station. Someone abandoned one, and we picked him up immediately."

"Oh, I'm going to go see," Ella said, back out into the chilly night before anyone could stop her.

While the other boys greeted their Gramma Finnie, Colleen inched closer to Daniel.

"I went to the square for Chloe's event, and I have to say, our Shane is marrying one dog lover of a great woman," Colleen said.

Daniel had to laugh. "Sure didn't start out that way when those two met."

"You mean when you *orchestrated* their meeting."

He rolled his eyes. "You, too, little sister?"

"Says the Dogfather." She winked. "Why deny it? You're a masterful, string-pulling matchmaker. Three down, three to go."

"I just give nudges, Collie. My kids do their own romancing." Of course, he gave *great* nudges.

Colleen turned so that her sons didn't hear her whisper, "Wish you'd work some of your matchmaking magic on my kids. At this rate, I'm never going to be a grandmother."

"Get in line. I still have Molly and Darcy to work on."

"And Aidan," Colleen reminded him. "Any word?" she added, hope in her voice.

"He's good and will call tomorrow."

The next set of lights brightened the drive and more right behind it, heralding the arrival of Daniel's kids, their significant others, and the few who made up the next generation.

In a matter of minutes, the kitchen was filled almost to capacity, the noise rising to the usual Christmas Eve frenzy, interrupted by barks as Rusty greeted his dog cousins Jag, Ruby, and Lola. Darcy's insane Shih Tzu, Kookie, ran circles around them all, adding to the chaos.

"Hi, Grandpa!" Pru, his thirteen-year-old granddaughter, gave Daniel a big kiss, followed by her mother, Molly.

"Merry Christmas, Dad," Molly murmured into a peck on his cheek.

He hugged his daughter extra tight and ran a hand over her thick brown waves, sensing that she'd been as restless lately as he had. Did Molly have the Christmas blues, too? "How's my girl?" he asked.

"Good, but what's this I hear about a Jack Russell left at the fire station?"

"He's being groomed."

"Without a complete physical?"

Daniel tipped his head and resisted a smile. "I think you forget who was the first veterinarian in this family."

"Oh yeah. You're just so, you know, retired. I mean from being a vet."

"I'm running the largest canine rescue and training facility in the state," he reminded her. "But I can check out a newbie. He's healthy, at least physically. But he's…" He shook his head, remembering how the pup had flinched at any touch. "Timid and agitated enough to make me suspect whoever left him should be punished. Severely."

She cringed, as they all would at the thought of an abused dog.

"All right, all right." Gramma Finnie clapped and raised her aging voice, but it was enough to bring down the volume and have everyone turn to their wee grandmother, the Irish lass who had started it all when she moved from County Waterford to Bitter Bark, North Carolina. "You all know what happens tonight."

"If you don't, I have the whole thing scheduled out," Pru said, sliding an arm around her grandmother, both of them about the same height and almost always next to each other at any family gathering.

"We know what to do on Christmas Eve," Liam, Daniel's oldest son, said.

"Yeah," Shane agreed. "You don't need to give marching orders, General Pru."

Pru's eyes, the same hazel color as her mother's and her "Grannie Annie" as she'd called her grandmother, widened at the peanut gallery comments. "We have some new people since last Christmas, thanks to some of the men in the family." She stood on her tiptoes and beamed at the three women who'd fallen for Liam, Shane, and Garrett.

"That was thoughtful of you, Pru," Garrett added, putting an arm around Jessie, the woman he'd be marrying on New Year's Eve. "I couldn't remember the exact order of events to tell Jessie."

"I suspected as much," Pru said, her gentle tease reminding them she might be the next generation and younger than all but Liam's new stepson, but she was probably the most organized and in control out of the whole lot. "First we light the Christmas candle and Gramma Finnie will tell us the entire Irish folklore behind it."

Someone groaned. Someone named Shane.

He earned a nudge from his fiancée, Chloe, and a sharp look from his grandmother.

"That means you want the long version, laddie?" Gramma demanded.

"Shut up, Shane," Liam mumbled to his brother, making their broad shoulders shake with laugher.

Pru waved off the interruption. "Then we have the gift exchange, my personal favorite part."

"Before Santa comes?" That small voice belonged to Christian, comfortably held high above the others on Liam's hip. Although he hadn't been formally adopted yet, Andi Rivers's six-year-old son was in every way Liam's boy now, and it had been that way since Andi and Liam had married right here in this house back in September.

"Oh, don't worry, Christian," Andi assured him, shooting a friendly warning look around the group to remind them there was a Santa-believing child in their midst again.

"This is just the gift exchange with our cousins," Liam told Christian. "Santa will come after we all go to sleep."

Everyone enthusiastically agreed to that, calming Christian's concerns.

"During gifts, we get a light snack," Pru said. "And then we go to Midnight Mass."

"Which is why we are all only allowed one drink during the first half," Shane whispered loudly to Chloe.

"After that, we get dinner, even though it's almost two in the morning!" Pru exclaimed, as if that was the most fun any family could possibly have.

And it had been at one time, Daniel thought as the unwanted grief bubbled up again. When Annie had been—

The kitchen door smacked open so hard, it felt like the old house shook. Darcy stood in the doorway, breathless, wearing nothing but a T-shirt and jeans, a grooming brush still in one hand.

"Jack Frost is gone!" she exclaimed.

"It's my fault!" Ella ran up behind her, swiping at the tears on her face. "I left the door to the grooming office open, and we turned and…"

"Shh, El. It's okay." Darcy, always the more mature of the two, quieted her cousin. "It's only been five minutes. He couldn't have gotten far."

Except they all knew that in five minutes, a dog could get lost in the hundred acres of Waterford Farm.

For one split second, everyone looked at Daniel, all wearing different expressions. Expectant, worried, even a little curious as to what his reaction would be. As if there would be any question, regardless of the date on the calendar or the schedule of events.

A dog was lost, and that changed everything.

"Break into groups of two and three," Daniel ordered, moving on instinct through a somewhat familiar drill. "Fan out over the entire property."

"Give that brush to Jag for a scent, Darcy," Liam added.

"Darcy, you patrol the kennel and central pen," Shane said. "He'll come to you before anyone else."

"I'll get treat bags," Garrett said, taking Jessie's hand to head out. "I can take a tractor down to the southern woods. Shane, you give Liam a ride on an ATV and take the northwest section. Mahoneys, circle the lake with Dad."

"I'll get flashlights." Darcy dragged a not-yet-calm Ella with her. "Come with me and stop fretting."

"Can I go?" Christian asked, hopping a bit as if he knew that request would be denied. "Jag's going!"

"I need you here with me, lad," Gramma said, scooting next to him. At his look of disappointment, she gave him a squeeze. "We man the central command center. It's the most important job of all."

"Oh...there's a central command center?"

"Right here next to the cookies," she said.

He stood a little straighter, appeased. "Okay. I can man that. What about Mommy?"

"She'll stay, too," Liam said.

Andi looked as stricken as her son at the idea. "I want to come with you."

Liam glanced down at his wife's stomach, still flat, but they all knew the precious cargo inside. "It's snowy and icy out there." He glanced to Shane for an assist and got one immediately.

"You three should stay," Shane said, putting a hand on Chloe's shoulder and nodding to Jessie. "You don't know the property like we do, and—"

"Are you kidding?" Chloe choked. "Not help find a lost dog?"

"I designed a house to be built on Liam's portion of the land," Andi said. "I've been out there a dozen or more times in the last two months."

"Of course we're coming with you," Jessie added, giving Garrett a look no man would argue with. "We're family, or about to be *in seven days*."

Liam, Shane, and Garrett shared silent looks, but Molly stepped in to referee. "Let them come along to each of your search sites," she said with what seemed like a little more force than necessary. "That's how my new sisters will learn the property and how to find a lost dog."

Daniel couldn't help noticing another exchange of looks between the three brothers, as if agreeing to something. To know how to pick their battles, Daniel hoped. It had been a bedrock of his happy marriage.

"All right," Shane said first.

"That's a plan," Garrett agreed.

"Let's go, then." Liam reached for Andi's hand, in concert with his brothers.

That decision made, everyone moved as a team, without a single complaint that Christmas took a backseat when a dog was lost. Ironically, no one would have appreciated or supported that more than Annie Kilcannon, Daniel thought.

Knowing she was watching down on her clan and her beloved farm, Daniel joined the Mahoney kids and headed into the snowy night to find Jack Frost.

Chapter Two

Liam helped Andi off the ATV at the bottom of one of the highest hills on Waterford Farm. With Jag in tow and Liam's innate knowledge of this land, it was the perfect place for them to do a thorough search.

"I'll call when we find him," Liam said, purposely sounding optimistic as he turned on an industrial-strength flashlight that would provide Jag with a light beam to follow. He'd need it since the moon was barely a sliver.

Shane revved the engine, anxious to go. "No, I'll call you when *we* find him." Of course his brother would make the dog hunt a competition he had to win.

"I just hope someone finds him." Chloe nestled closer to Shane and rubbed her hands together. "Nothing worries me more than a lost dog."

"No fear, babe," Shane assured her as he rumbled away and left Liam and Andi to follow Jag. "We got this."

The muscular German shepherd was trained as a *Schutzhund*, which made him a better protector than tracker, but his nose was powerful, and Liam was certain that he'd find *any* living thing out here.

They trudged through the snowfall everyone had been so excited about the day before, but a white Christmas seemed like icy danger now.

"You shouldn't even be out here," Liam said, gripping Andi tighter.

"I'm fine, really."

"You're barely twelve weeks pregnant."

"Which is not a handicap," she reminded him. "I'm being careful, and I know every inch of this area. I was out here with a surveyor a few days ago before any snow fell. Jag is just about to come to a rise in the ground."

Almost immediately, the dog stepped up and then down, exactly as she'd said.

Still, Liam held her close and scanned the untouched snow of the hill where, come spring, they'd break ground for their own family home that Andi, a skilled architect, had designed.

"I still think you should have stayed with Gramma Finnie and Christian."

She elbowed him on a laugh. "We've passed three months, and I'm healthy as a horse." She grinned up at him. "And as hungry as one. Or maybe I could eat one. Can't remember the phrase, but in this case, they both work."

He unsnapped his parka pocket and pulled out one of the three protein bars he never went anywhere without. For her, not him. "Figured you'd get starved."

"Oh." She took it and looked up at him like he'd just handed her the crown jewels. "I'd marry you all over again, Liam Kilcannon."

"Don't tempt me. It was the best night of my life."

She pressed closer and unwrapped the bar. "I admit I got a little panicked when Pru said 'light snack.' Wondered what everyone else was going to eat. Think the dog might smell this bar and come to us?"

He shook his head, watching Jag move with purpose. "The others will use treats or special whistles to get the dog, but we have Jag, and if there's a dog out here, he'll sniff that little pupper out from his hiding place."

"Sad we don't even know his real name, but we could try common ones. Rover! Spot!" She smiled up at him. "What's another good dog name?"

"I like Anne."

She stopped midstep and blinked at him. "That's a good dog name?"

"It's a good *daughter* name."

"Oooh." She let out a sigh. "That's what's on your mind?"

"Always," he admitted. "I can't stop thinking about this baby for one minute."

"I know, I'm the same way." She chewed contentedly as they followed Jag's black silhouette in the light, watching him sniff side to side, but continuing his climb to the top of the hill.

In the distance, they heard the barely audible calls of his siblings, and the deep, baritone bark of Einstein, who'd gone with Declan and Connor.

"Do you think they found him?" Andi asked, excitement making her voice rise.

"No."

"How can you be sure?"

"That bark is too steady and calm to be the sound

191

of a hound who found his target," he told her. "What about the name?"

She smiled up at the return to the baby subject. "Anne is your mother's name. I kind of love that idea," she said. "But I don't know if there could ever be another Anne Kilcannon."

"No, she was one of a kind, for sure." Liam closed his eyes for a second, letting her memory hit. "No one loved Christmas like my mother. Every tradition is hers."

"Even that candle Pru was talking about?"

"Oh, no. The Christmas candle in the window is all Gramma Finnie, straight from Ireland, like she is. But my mom made sure every annual tradition was kept alive, that we always did the little things that make Christmas the same every year."

"I want to keep those traditions in our home, Liam," she said. "Which will be right..." She broke away and jogged a few steps before tapping her boot on the snow. "Here. This is where our front door will be."

"Wow, you *do* know your way around this hill." He joined her at the rise and took a moment to do a slow three-sixty scan with his light. The beam highlighted the snow-trimmed trees and winter hills, making them look desolate, but beautiful. It would be a jaw-dropper of a view from their front window.

"See any tracks?" she asked.

"There's no sign that dog was out here," he said. "Tracks would be fresh."

"Want to go down the other side of the hill?" she asked.

"No, no. Too steep for you."

Even in the moonlight, he could see in her expression that she didn't agree. "Go with Jag and check. I'll wait here."

He considered that for a moment, then shook his head. "We'll look from up here and watch Jag."

"What if the little puppy runs away?"

"He won't." Liam snapped his fingers twice, and Jag instantly stopped and turned, waiting for his master's instructions. "Down there, boy," he pointed, emphasizing the command by moving the flashlight. "In the trees and bushes."

Jag didn't hesitate, but loped across the hill, kicking up snow and following the light beam down the hill into a small grouping of trees.

"Will he stay in sight?"

"Unless he smells something," Liam said, taking a few steps, his gaze locked on the dog, ready to give him the next command. But Jag sniffed dutifully, rounding the trees and poking his mighty snout in the bushes, while Liam and Andi scanned the landscape, looking for anything that might move, bark, run, or hide.

In the meantime, Liam wanted to go back to the subject that interested him most. "What about Anne as a middle name?"

"Oooh." Andi nodded. "I like that. Especially since Anne is so close to my name, anyway."

"True."

"Look, Jag just went into those shrubs."

Liam peered at the spot, certain the dog would be in and out in a second. "But it could be a boy," he said.

"We'll know in ten days," she reminded him. "Unless you want to be surprised."

"I think—"

Jag's bark cut him off, loud and insistent. "Whoa," Liam said, putting a hand up to stop Andi as she took a step in that direction. "Let him come out."

"But the dog could run away!" she exclaimed.

"He won't."

Jag's bark hit high gear, and Liam still couldn't see him. Was something wrong?

"Go, Liam."

He had to. Without giving it much more thought, Liam took off down the hill, still unable to see the dog, though he could follow his voice.

"Jag!" He slipped on some snow, but easily caught himself.

"Be careful, Liam!"

He held up a hand, which he realized she probably couldn't see because he'd taken the flashlight, but zipped down in the direction of Jag's furious barks.

"Watch out, there's a sharp drop off a ledge—"

He didn't hear the rest. He went flying through the air and felt the protein bars *and* his phone pop out of his pocket. His first thought? How in the name of all that was holy could he be *that* stupid?

His second one was how did Andi know their property better than he did?

And his third one, as he landed with a thud and felt his foot twist, was that he'd sprained his damn ankle. Which took him back to his first thought. *Stupid.*

Chapter Three

"Did you hear that?" Jessie asked Garrett as they reached the edge of the woods that covered a good ten acres of the southern section of Waterford Farm.

"No, but that's why we have to be very, very quiet." Garrett put his finger to his lips and whispered, "The quieter we are, the better chance we have of hearing the dog."

"But did you hear that noise?" she asked, matching his breathy volume.

"You think it was a dog?"

"I think it was…" She peered into the darkness, her jaw tight and a lip trapped under her teeth. "Something."

Garrett put his arm around his fiancée and tugged her closer. "Don't worry, Little Red Riding Hood. There are no wolves in these woods."

"But there are foxes and possums and…" She shivered. "Ghosts?"

He chuckled softly. "Like Christmas Past and Future?"

"Like…" She slowed her step as they neared the first bit of cleared brush that led to a path few people on earth knew as well as Garrett Kilcannon. "Ghosts."

He kissed her head and took a second to inhale the smell of winter and woods that clung to her reddish-gold hair. "I've been in these woods a zillion times. It was one of my favorite Manhunt hiding places because my sisters didn't have the nerve to come in here."

"Exactly. Because it's creepy."

"Not with me. And do you remember the best game of Manhunt ever?" He pulled her closer and mouthed the rest into her ear. "I won the game *and* the woman I love."

Her smile returned, normally bright at the mention of the night they'd gotten engaged while hiding in a tree, looked shaky. "That was near the lake within plain sight of the house," Jessie said. "Why didn't we take that section to find Jack Frost?"

"Because it's easy and familiar, so it made sense for my dad to lead my cousins there. But I know every white oak and longleaf pine in here, and especially where the poison ivy lurks. This is, as we say in North Carolina, *mah neck of mah woods*." He layered on his Southern accent, knowing it always made her smile.

But she sighed instead, leaning into him as if she were still battling some fears. "Is there an actual path we can follow?"

"Yup." He pointed his flashlight at the thin dusting of snow and ice, and what, to an untrained eye, would look like, well, snow and ice. "See the path?"

"No, I don't."

He scraped some snow with his boot. "This is a path, I promise. Hold my hand and come with me." He pulled her closer for a kiss. "Could be fun."

"We're supposed to be hunting for a dog."

"We are. We just have to be very quiet and listen for any sounds." He lowered his voice to a whisper. "So kiss quietly."

She gave him a warning look, but relented and kissed him back. "I can't believe we'll be married in one week," she whispered against his lips.

He let out a little groan of pure pleasure. "Believe it."

They held each other's gaze for a moment. "I love you so much, Jessica Jane," Garrett whispered.

"I know, and I love you, but we need to find a dog."

"We will. The dog will come to us. Dogs come to me. And you," he reminded her. "Remember the first time you met Lola?" He inhaled noisily, poking his nose in Jessie's hair and knit scarf. "Love at first sniff. For both of us."

She angled her head and practically purred at his touch, then that turned into a moan. "Oh, Lola. That just reminds me the book isn't finished yet, and I wanted to get it done before the wedding."

He curled an arm around her and moved them forward in slow, silent unison, knowing that talking— well, whispering—about the book she was writing would get her mind off being scared and cold.

"*For the Love of Lola* is going to be a masterpiece," he said softly. "When you changed the perspective to Lola's voice? Sheer genius."

She snuggled closer in gratitude. "I just want to tell her story and combine it with the history of Waterford Farm in a way that will make readers fall in love with Lola and this amazing place."

"It's money in the bank, babe. For you and Waterford." He truly believed that when her book was published, it would be a best seller. "Not only will it drive more canine training business, it's going to promote rescuing dogs, which, as you know, is what matters most to me." He added a kiss. "After my soon-to-be wife."

"I hope so. But let's find that dog, Garrett."

"We are. We're spreading our scent. He'll come closer and we'll hear him. Listen."

They took a few steps, then stopped as Garrett carefully examined every bush and tree, peering into the shadows in case anything moved.

"How deep into the sinister woods should we go?" Jessie asked.

Garrett chuckled. "Sinister. You're such a wordsmith."

"What would you call them? Bright, cheery, and friendly?"

"I call them home," he assured her. "I could find my way in and out of here blindfolded. Let's go over here." He tugged her toward the creek bed. "If the water isn't frozen, he might be getting a drink."

"Good idea. Unless the ghosts are thirsty, too."

"No ghosts, Jess." He glanced at her, his heart shifting around as it always did when he looked into those green eyes. Jessica Jane Curtis came into his life to "expose" him to the world, and she'd done nothing but heal ancient wounds. "But I will not lose you or let you get hurt. Ever."

She dropped her head on his shoulder, but then suddenly jerked away. "Did you hear that?"

He shook his head and made himself very still,

closing his eyes to zero in on sound over every other sense.

"Listen." She inched back. "I heard something. That."

A chilly breeze rustled a thousand dry leaves, sending a few of them to the ground and a shiver over Jessie.

"That was wind," he assured her. "Not a dog."

"Or..." She wiggled her fingers in front of her face and made a woo-woo sound.

He laughed again. "You're ridiculous, and there are..."

He heard it then, the sound of a twig cracking, then the brush of feet against leaves.

"Oh boy," she whispered, hugging herself a little. "Definitely Casper."

No, but it could be a bird, a deer, a possum...or even a sly fox.

"This way." He gestured toward the sound, shining the flashlight beam for her to follow. But in less than twenty steps, brush covered the path, making it impossible to navigate.

Garrett pursed his lips and made a kissing noise, one most dogs would recognize as a call. "Here, little one," he called loudly, snapping his fingers twice. "Come."

They both turned at another rustling sound.

"There!" Jessie said, but whatever it was took off at the sound of her voice, cracking more branches and moving leaves. "Oh." She put her hand over her mouth. "I scared it into the bushes."

"I'll go in there. Don't move." He took a few steps forward, reaching into his pocket for gloves, not to protect him from the cold, but because he knew these shrubs had thistles and thorns.

"Garrett!" Jessie called softly. "He's back there." She pointed in the complete other direction than where he was headed. Then another stirring of leaves where the original sound had been.

They looked at each other in dismay. "I heard it," Jessie said, pointing one way.

"And I heard it over here," Garrett replied, pointing the other.

Then they both heard sounds in both directions, growing more distant.

"I'm going with this one," Garrett said, indicating the sound closest to him.

"But that other one could be the dog." She reached for the flashlight. "Let me look for one, and you look for the other."

"That's not a good idea."

"Garrett! You just said you could find your way through the woods blindfolded. Give me the flashlight."

So he had, and he could. He relented and handed over the flashlight. "Don't go more than twenty feet, and come right back. Promise?"

She nodded solemnly, taking the flashlight. "As if I want to be alone in the haunted forest."

"You have your phone?"

She made a face. "I left my purse at the house."

"Here, take mine." He dug in his pocket for it. "Or you could just stay right here, Jessie. I'll find one animal and—"

"The other will be gone. We *have* to find that dog," she insisted. "I can do it."

"Okay," he agreed. "Twenty feet, no more."

Once again, an animal snapped a twig on their right, while another one pushed some brush on their left. The one closer to Garrett sounded a little bigger. He had to get it out of here before it scared Jessie. With one last look, they turned and walked in opposite directions.

Garrett moved by the light coming from Jessie's direction, but in seconds, the woods were bathed in darkness. He followed instinct and the sound of an animal darting through the trees, skipping over the path, silent on the snow.

He followed it left, then right, then round an old live oak he always climbed for Manhunt.

He stopped to listen, not hearing anything...not even Jessie. Then the sound of a footfall behind him made him turn, but whatever it was shot off in Jessie's direction.

Garrett followed, stopping just to listen, then going deeper and deeper into the woods, a little out of familiar territory, but as long as the creek was on his left, he knew he could find his way back.

Fifty paces, then a hundred, then a turn, then the path stopped and...so did he, listening for any sound, especially the soft trickle of water.

Nothing.

Was the creek frozen? He headed that way, but...*damn it*. He was nowhere near the creek. Nowhere near a tree, stone, clearing, or landmark he recognized. He turned around, without a phone or a light, and stared back in the direction he thought he'd come from as a cold, sickening fear worked up his spine.

Jessie.

"Jess!" he shouted, his voice breaking the silence, but there was no echo. Not with this much snow and this many trees. "Jessie! Flash your light, so I can find you."

But he didn't hear a thing except the rustle of leaves.

He was lost in his own neck of the woods, and the woman he loved was alone and terrified. His siblings, one in particular, would have a ball with this turn of events on a night they'd expected to be so very merry.

Chapter Four

Shane turned off the tractor and stared at the snow-covered road ahead. "You ready for an uphill hike in the snow, Miami girl?"

"To find this dog?" Chloe was already scrambling off the tractor. "Of course. I have boots on."

"But no gloves."

She held up her bare hands. "I always forget them. And the scarf. There's so many extra parts to winter."

Still seated, Shane looked down at her, affection pulling at his heart. "I'll hold your hands, or we can run back and get you a pair. You know I never wear them."

"Because you can't feel the dogs with them on," she said, knowing exactly why he, a professional trainer, wouldn't wear gloves. "So I don't want them. I won't be able to grab that little puppy when I catch sight of him."

He had to laugh, climbing down. "And I thought I wanted to win bad. My competitive nature must be contagious."

"Not a bit, but your dog-loving nature is." She reached for his hand, tucking her fingers up his sleeve.

"I will not sleep tonight if someone doesn't bring that dog home, Shane."

"Someone will. Count on it." He tugged her closer and kissed her lips long enough to make them a little warmer, then drew back and angled his head toward the snowy trail ahead. "Do you recognize this place?"

She paused to look up the grade of the hill. "Is this what you guys call Mud Road?" She threw him a smile. "Of course I recognize it. The sight of our first real make-out session. Pretty sure some clothes came off."

He grinned back, remembering the day he got Chloe Somerset on an ATV and in her first mud bath. It might have been the moment he realized he loved this beautiful, thin-blooded neat freak.

"'Fraid you'll have to keep your top on tonight," he said. "It's freezing-ass cold. And there are probably ice patches, so we have to go up on foot this time."

"Of course, we don't want to scare off the little pupper." She rubbed her hands together, blowing on them. "I can't stand the thought of that dog out here in the cold, Shane. Let's go. We have to find little Jack Frost."

"Okay, no worries, I have a plan." Taking her hand, they set off for the hill, staying in the center where the snow wasn't much more than a crunchy dusting under their boots.

"Tell me the plan," she said as they hiked.

"We get to the lookout at the top first, and keep our clothes on, even though if we weren't looking for a lost dog..." He pulled her in for a sexy, slow kiss. "We could find creative ways to warm up."

"Mmm. And let someone else find the dog?"

He considered that. "Might be worth losing." He kissed her again, letting their tongues touch and heat up. "But who cares about winning, anyway?" He deepened the kiss, tasting mint and snow and this woman he loved so intensely.

"Who are you?" she teased, pulling back to reluctantly end the contact they both enjoyed so much.

"Me? You're the former Florida germophobe out in the freezing cold ready to get snow and dirt all over you." But the truth was, they'd both changed since falling in love.

"I am Chloe Somerset...Kilcannon, as of April eighteenth." She smiled up at him. "Your wife."

"Damn, that sounds good." He slipped an arm around her and lowered for one more kiss, but she drew back.

"Shane. The *dog*."

Oh yeah, right.

"What is your plan?" she asked.

"Okay, the plan. We go to the lookout, which is the highest point on all of Waterford Farm. The entire way up this hill, we'll strategically drop treats to lead the dog to us."

"Treats. Genius."

He pulled out the bag and let a few tiny cookies fall. "Of course, because I'm the dog trainer. Garrett wants to rescue them all, so he'll try to get the pooch to come to him. Liam wants to turn them into watchdogs, so he'll use Jag to do his work. But I know how a dog thinks."

"Affection above all, then food and fun," she said, reciting something she'd heard him say a hundred times with the dogs at Waterford. "Okay, give me some treats to strategically drop, too. But not too many. We want that dog to be hungry and follow us up to where he can't get out of our sight."

He grinned at her. "You do pay attention when I train the dogs."

"Mostly I watch the trainer," she admitted, blowing on her hands again. "God, when am I going to learn about gloves?"

"I got you some for Christmas."

"Really? Too bad we didn't do the present exchange first. I might have worn them. Anything else?"

"Do you want me to ruin the surprise? Not a chance," he said. "What did you get me?"

"Coal, because you're a bad boy."

"Which is what you love most about me."

"Maybe. And I'd love you more if you tell me what else you got me."

"No way." He hugged her a little tighter. "I want it to be a surprise, so don't keep asking. It's good. You'll love it."

"Give me a hint," she urged.

"Okay," he agreed. "It's lace, skimpy, and able to be removed with my teeth."

"You better not make me open that at the gift exchange, Shane Kilcannon."

"I have to. You know Gramma Finnie will take a picture and blog about it."

That just made her laugh again, a sound that rang as sweet as any Christmas carols. They walked without talking for a few minutes, listening to their steps on the snow and dirt, then they heard the bark of a distant dog, one that sounded pretty excited.

"That was Jag," he said, instantly recognizing the dog he'd spent several months helping Liam train.

"He found Jack Frost?" She stopped and grabbed his arm.

"He'll call home if he has, then Gramma will call all of us or send out a group text. Just in case, let's keep going."

"So you've done this before, I take it."

Shane laughed. "Find a lost dog? My whole life. Not on Christmas Eve, though. That's a first."

"I bet your mom would not be happy about this interruption of her traditions."

"This one?" He shook his head, fighting a smile, thinking of his mother. "She'd be all over this one, trust me."

He felt Chloe's gaze scrutinizing him.

"What?" he asked when she didn't say anything.

"Nothing, it's just that you've come so far with your grief."

He dropped a treat, slowing his steps, thinking about that statement. "You've helped," he said simply. "I'm not mad at her at all anymore."

"Your dad is suffering, though."

"I know that. We all know that," he said. "He thinks he's doing such a magnificent job of covering it up, but Christmas was Mom's big thing. This time of year has to be hard on him, especially when all three of his sons—well, the three that are home—have someone to share it with."

"But that makes him happy," she said. "He's the Dogfather, remember? The driving force behind love in this family."

She took a treat and gave him a questioning look.

When he nodded, she dropped it like the two little lost kids in one of the fairy tales his mother used to read to him. "He needs love, too," he said, the words surprising him even as they came out.

"Then his kids ought to turn the tables on him and set him up with some women."

"Oh, no." Shane shook his head vehemently. "He's not going to remarry. That'll never happen. He'll never even date."

She choked softly. "He's sixty and sexy. Not dead and done."

"Enough with the tourism phrases," he said, trying for a light note but failing. "This isn't a town you're selling to America, it's my *dad*."

She didn't argue, but Shane knew Chloe well enough to know that didn't mean the end of the discussion.

But then the hill got so steep that she had to concentrate on each step, while she held his hand and worked to catch her breath, which came out in quick puffs of white clouds. Just as they reached the lookout, he put the treat bag on the snow, holding on to one. Once they were situated at the top of the hill, he pulled out his phone to make sure he hadn't missed a call or text.

"Do we still have a chance to win?" she asked.

"I hope someone found him. Then we have a chance to…" He angled his head toward the ground. "Make snow angels."

Her mouth opened in a sweet little 'o.' "I've never done that."

"Sand angels in Miami?"

"I have an idea, though." She wrapped her arms

around his waist and looked up at him. "I was thinking of something."

"Yes?"

"Why don't you make fixing up the Dogfather a family competition? Then you'll get into the idea."

For a split second, he considered it, then stomped that stupid idea away. "No way, I'm not—"

Something small and dark darted in and out of his peripheral vision. Chloe must have seen it to, because she spun around. "Oh, what are we doing? We should be looking for that dog!"

He didn't answer, but she pointed to the left.

"Over there!" She started after the tiny dark spot, which was too far away for Shane to see clearly. She pounced, sending up a cloud of snow, but Shane saw it shoot away, still out of the beam of his light and impossible to really see.

"Go get him, Shane!"

On instinct, he launched forward in the direction of the shadow, throwing himself down in a drift, only to come up empty-handed.

"I see him." Chloe whizzed by, down the hill a ways, but she slid onto her butt and let out a shriek as she took a sled ride minus the sled. "Oh! Go get him, Shane! Get him!"

He'd have laughed if he wasn't so damn focused on not looking like a fool in front of her, or not seeming to care about the dog. "I got him!"

The animal disappeared under a bush about twenty feet away from where Chloe had stopped. Still holding one treat, Shane headed in that direction, pausing to give Chloe a hand up, then the two of them clomped through the snow toward the bush.

"We got him now," Chloe whispered.

He very much doubted that, but he neared the bush, his treat extended, not entirely sure what he'd find under there, but he had a pretty good idea. "Come here....*Jack*. Come here, boy."

Under the bush, something moved, uncertain.

"Shane."

"Shh. Shh. I got this."

"But Shane."

He shook his head, focused, ignoring the cold snow on the knees of his pants, one hundred percent intent on proving to her that he could do this.

"*Shane.*"

Shane crouched and slid his hand into the bush, palm up. As the tiny mouth pressed against his skin, he swooped in with his other hand and closed it around the little furry body, half expecting to be nipped.

Victorious, he pulled out...a tiny brown and white bunny. "As I suspected...not Jack Frost. Jack *Rabbit.*"

"Shane." Chloe jabbed his arm, and he looked up to follow the beam of the flashlight she held.

There, at the top of the hill, was an ornery-looking raccoon, munching contentedly on the treats they'd left behind and staring at them like they held his dessert.

"Put the bunny in your pocket, Shane."

"What?" He glanced at her. "Why?"

"To keep it safe from that predator."

"It's a wild rabbit, Chloe, and while I appreciate your newfound love of all animals, this one should stay out here. It knows how to fend for itself."

She looked at him like he was out of his mind. "That raccoon will devour it."

"Probably not." He gave the little fur ball a pet. "They know how to handle their environment."

"We're bringing him home." She tipped her head and gave him a look he'd never say no to. "Please."

Very carefully, he tucked the tiny rabbit into his pocket and sighed. "I'll never hear the end of this from my brothers," he murmured.

Chapter Five

"Somebody should have called or texted by now." Pru looked at her phone for the twentieth time since she and Molly had circled the large training area behind the classroom, shining flashlights, dropping treats, and listening for sounds of life.

Somebody sure should have, Molly thought. "Dad probably doesn't want to give up," she said. "But if you're cold, honey, you should go back in with Gramma and Christian."

"I'm not a kid anymore," Pru said. "I don't need to be at the 'central command center eating cookies.'"

Normally, that would be funny, since Pru most certainly *was* a kid and she knew that Gramma Finnie was just making the moment palatable for a little boy on Christmas. But Molly detected an edge in her daughter's voice, one that had been there a little too frequently the past few weeks, one that Molly didn't really like or understand. But maybe it was the holiday or…hormones. She was thirteen, after all. PMS couldn't be that far away.

"Well, you kind of are still a kid," Molly said. "And this isn't exactly how you want to spend Christmas Eve. Plus, it's cold."

"I don't care about cold," she muttered.

"We might give up earlier than we normally would," Molly suggested, knowing there was no *might* about it. "Otherwise, we won't have time for gifts and…what's after that? A 'light snack,' as you put it."

"Who cares?"

Molly stopped dead in her tracks at the question. "Are you turning into a smartass for Christmas, or are you unhappy with this particular turn of events?"

Pru closed her eyes, not answering the rare reprimand.

Yes, she'd turned thirteen this year, and yes, that made her a bona fide teenager. But nothing about Molly's daughter had ever been cliché or standard. Pru had been born amazing, mature, organized…good. She'd never given Molly a moment's heartache, so why would she start on Christmas Eve?

Finally, Pru lifted a shoulder. "Whatever, Mom."

Oh boy. She'd just gotten *whatevered*, and that couldn't go unnoticed. It was nothing short of a cry for help coming from this girl.

"Prudence Anne Kilcannon. What is going on with you?"

Silent, Pru kicked some snow, then made a show of looking through the fence to the training area they'd just circled.

Molly's heart dropped, and an ancient—well, thirteen-year-old—fear resurfaced. Was this the day she'd be confronted? How much longer until Pru demanded to know who her father was and why Molly hadn't married him or even mentioned his name? The question, the conversation, the truth—or whatever version of it Molly decided to use—loomed large.

Not on Christmas Eve. Please, Pru. Not on Christmas Eve.

But what better time than when sentiments ran high and questions about family must hang heavy in a young girl's head? She'd ask any minute, Molly just knew it. Would she be soft-spoken? Demanding? Tearful? How would she broach the subject, and how would Molly answer?

With the truth of course, difficult as that may be.

But couldn't someday *not* be today?

"January's coming," Pru said, earning a weird look from Molly.

"As it often does after December."

"January is a month of new beginnings." Pru kicked a little puff of sand.

Oh, the roundabout technique. Not Pru's usual approach to a problem, but one Molly recognized. "We should make some *reservations*." Molly grinned at her, knowing Pru would remember their inside joke of what five-year-old Pru called 'resolutions.'

But Pru didn't smile back. "Speaking of months, by my calculations, I was conceived in November." Oh, Lord. Forget roundabout. She was going dead-on now. "Am I right?"

She most certainly was. The night after Thanksgiving, fourteen years ago. Molly swallowed, silent.

"And you were nineteen."

"Gee, and here I thought math wasn't your best subject."

"Then how about science? I could have a DNA test, you know. I looked into it. Obviously, I have your eyes but not your hair. I mean, I know a test wouldn't tell me my father's name or—"

"Really, Pru? On Christmas Eve?" The question came out knife-sharp, lashing in self-defense.

"Well, it's not a normal Christmas Eve." No longer interested in the dog or the party or the messed-up schedule of events that had mattered so much, Pru pushed back her thick, nearly black hair. Hair that had none of Molly's curls or hints of red. Hair that looked exactly like her father's.

"Are you ever going to tell me?" she demanded.

Of course. Someday. Not tonight. Not yet. "There's not much to tell."

Pru made a dramatic fake cough. "Well, there was enough to produce *me*."

Ire shot up Molly's spine, even though she knew it was wrong and Pru had every right to ask questions that Molly had managed to avoid and ignore for more than thirteen years. The only person on earth who'd known the truth was Annie Kilcannon, and Molly had no doubt that her mother had taken the secret to her grave.

Mom had sworn she wouldn't even tell Dad, and Molly had believed her.

With Mom's help, Molly had been able to fend off all questions from her father, siblings, or townsfolk, and after a while, they'd either forgotten or just let it drop.

Whatever "mistake" Molly had made, the result

was Pru, a sparkling, amazing, delightful addition to the family and, until Liam adopted Christian, the only grandchild of a very big clan. Molly's mistake, her bad choice and poor timing, had turned into a blessing that no one would ever give up. Exactly as Mom had promised it would.

Wasn't that enough for Pru?

But Pru didn't ever let anything drop, especially if it wasn't done according to plan. And nothing about her conception was *planned*. As Molly often joked in a way to shut down questions, she'd named her daughter Prudence because she hadn't exercised any to get her. She never wanted anyone to think Pru was the result of an unwanted advance.

On the contrary, Molly had wanted it very, very much. Regret hadn't set in until later, when he disappeared and Molly cried in her bathroom on New Year's Day, the life she'd planned gone as she looked at a thin pink line on a stick. Her heart hammered with an old, but still tender, ache.

"Not tonight, Pru, please." Molly's voice cracked, and Pru slowed her step, her green-brown eyes, so much like Molly's, softening just a little. She might want answers, but she loved her mother. That would be the battle Pru had to wage in her heart, and Molly knew it.

"Then when, Mom?" Pru put her hand on Molly's shoulder. "Just tell me when."

"Next year."

She smiled just enough to reveal a peek of braces and her selection of red and green bands to celebrate the holiday. "That's in a week."

Damn. "So it is."

Pru huffed out a breath and made a show of looking for the dog. "Kids at school ask."

Oh God. Of course they did. "And what do you tell them?"

"That it's none of their business."

"Damn right it isn't."

"But it's *my* business," Pru insisted in a harsh whisper. "It's all I think about."

"Oh." The word came out like a jagged sigh as Molly put her arm around her. "I…I know you deserve the truth, but this isn't the right time, Pru."

Her daughter's eyes filled with tears that had nothing to do with the cold. "Just give me a date and a time."

"That you were conceived?"

"That you'll tell me. Everything. Every single thing."

She might be too young for that much detail. "I have an idea," Molly said. "After Christmas, when things settle into normal, why don't you and I make a reservation?"

"Mom, I get the joke. I said reservation for resolution. You can stop that now."

"No, I mean a *reservation*. Somewhere away. The beach, maybe? The Outer Banks is gorgeous in the winter, and we can take a weekend away, just the two of us. We'll talk, and I'll tell you everything, answer every question, and I'll be completely honest." She wanted to be, and frankly, it would be a relief.

"Okay, but—"

"Hey, you guys!"

They both turned, seeing Darcy and Ella running toward them across the training field.

"Did they find him?" Pru asked. "Do we have Jack Frost?"

"No," Ella said, her shoulders dropping in an over-the-top dramatic sigh. "Gramma Finnie called off the search."

"Gramma Finnie?" Pru drew back. "It's Grandpa who is supposed to do that."

Molly and Darcy shared a look, knowing she was right. "But it's Christmas Eve," Molly said. "Gramma's taking over tonight."

"Are we absolutely sure we can't find that dog?" Pru's voice rose in a wail. "He may not survive the night!"

"Oh, he will," Darcy assured her, giving Molly a look that only a big sister could interpret—genuine guilt. "He's a hearty little fellow, right, Ella?"

"Absolutely. I know we'll find him when the sun comes up."

That seemed to appease Pru, who let herself be folded into a hug from her aunt Darcy.

"I hope so," Pru said on a sigh, including Ella in the embrace. "I hope we'll find him Christmas morning. Can you imagine how awesome that will be?"

Molly's heart nearly burst with love at the words. She watched these three women she loved so intensely hug and support each other, and the emotion nearly made her dizzy.

Did Pru have to know the other side of her gene pool when this one was so, so good? It wasn't like she could ever have a relationship with her father. Would that be the hardest part of the conversation? Not just who he was, but what had happened to him?

Guess she'd find out in January, the month of new beginnings.

"Come on, Mom." Pru swept an arm around Molly and added a kiss on the cheek, which was warm and conciliatory, as if she were satisfied with their plan. "Let's try to save what we can of Christmas Eve. For the family. For Grandpa. He's sad about Grannie Annie, can't you tell?"

"Oh yes, Pru, we all know." Molly hugged her daughter, and let the pang of missing her mother hit a little harder than usual. How she longed to have Annie Kilcannon to help guide her through these years the way she did with the first ten years of Pru's life. "How did you ever get such a good heart?"

Pru pressed her lips to Molly's ear. "Who knows? Maybe I inherited it from my mystery father."

Molly heard the tease in her voice, but knew it wasn't a joke. She inched back and looked her daughter in the eyes. "Next year, I promise."

"I can't wait."

But Molly could. January.

But now, on a night that was supposed to be merry and bright, she had this sword hanging over her head. Well, she had until January…and then she'd have to tell her daughter the truth that her father had disappeared…without a trace.

Chapter Six

Daniel returned to the house first, warmed up for a few minutes, then returned to the kitchen to wait for the search parties to show up. They came into the house in pairs, one sadder than the next, which just added to Daniel's general malaise and his sense that this might be the worst Christmas in Kilcannon history.

Declan and Connor Mahoney stomped snow off their booted feet and grumbled about how they damn near went through the ice on the lake after Daniel had headed back home at Gramma's insistence.

"Hope that dog didn't," Daniel said as he offered them a choice of eggnog or whiskey. No surprise, they both chose whiskey.

"That dog's not in the lake, Uncle Daniel," Connor assured him, his deep-blue eyes as serious and intense as he was. "And if he was, I'da made Declan jump in after him."

His brother snorted and knocked back the whiskey. "And I'd have done it for you, Uncle D," Declan said, giving a broad grin. "You know I'd do anything for you."

Touched, Daniel patted their sturdy shoulders and ushered the young men into the living room, turning to the doorway to greet Ella and Darcy, who were still writhing in guilt. Or maybe giggling. Sometimes, even as grown women, he couldn't tell. Of course, in his eyes, they were still little girls, although he knew neither of these thirty-year-olds was a *girl* anymore.

"I'm so sorry, Dad," Darcy said, shoving bedraggled blond hair from her angelic face. Darcy had always been the most stunningly beautiful Kilcannon, and that was saying a lot with his kids. She had Annie's fine features and her sweet smile.

And all Daniel wanted right then was to see that smile again. "Honey, stop berating yourself. Mistakes happen."

She gave him a look. "Kilcannons don't lose dogs."

"A Mahoney did," Ella said, hanging her head like a miserable hound. "I just want to die."

"That would only make matters worse," Daniel said, giving his niece a hug. "Gramma has notified the sheriff and fire department and, of course, she'll post something on social media."

They each gave a dry laugh. The fact that the oldest member of the family had the most active online presence never ceased to be amusing.

"So why don't you two grab something to drink, go change, and let it go for Christmas Eve?" Daniel suggested. "Not everyone is back yet. Shane or Garrett or Liam could walk in here carrying that pup any minute."

"My money's on Shane," Ella said.

Darcy looked over her shoulder, genuine worry in

her eyes. "But where are they all? Didn't Gramma Finnie call and tell them to come home?"

"I think so," he said. "Go on, ladies. It's time for you to have a little fun."

But they moped out of the room just as Molly and Pru came up to the door, arm in arm, their heads close as they talked. Those two were something, he thought with a smile. Their relationship was pure and special and...different.

He opened the door to welcome them with a hug.

When he held Molly, he felt her shudder a little, as if the whole ordeal had been too much. He inched back as Pru slipped away to join the others.

"You okay, Moll?" Daniel asked, searching her face and not loving the unhappiness there.

"Sure, Dad. Just frustrated we didn't find him and..." She swallowed and closed her eyes. "I miss Mom, too. She always knew the right thing to do or say."

That punched his gut as he pulled her in for another hug. "If it's any consolation, you have her heart and soul, Molly. She's always watching you and sending you help from heaven."

"Good, 'cause I'm going to need it."

Daniel frowned, trying to figure out what was bothering her. And then he knew. All three of her brothers had found love in the last six months, and that had to have exposed a raw nerve that she was facing a life alone. She always seemed to embrace that, but tonight she seemed different.

He knew exactly what had to be done. Some matchmaking. But who could be good enough for his Molly? No mere mortal, that was for sure.

He kissed her forehead and nudged her toward the living room, hoping the family and Christmas, even this mess of a Christmas, would work its magic on her.

Then he returned to the kitchen door to stare out at the shadows of Waterford Farm. From here, he could see the kennels and outbuildings of the canine business and beyond to the classrooms, training pens, and toward the path that led to the lake, creek, and acres of woods, mud roads, and hills.

That dog was out there somewhere, and it damn near broke his heart to think about. He closed his eyes and pictured the tan and white face he'd examined late that afternoon, remembering the fear that darkened the pup's eyes and the way he quivered even when being handled gently on the exam table. Poor Jack Frost.

When he opened his eyes, he saw a shadow move from behind the kennels, then two people emerge arm in arm. Was that Shane and Chloe? They held something between them, close to Chloe's chest. Daniel's heart kicked up, but as they stepped into the light from the porch, he could see it wasn't a dog, but a…bunny?

He opened the door for them, and Chloe looked up. "This might be more appropriate for Easter, Dr. K," she said. "Shane has caught us a rabbit, but no dog."

Shane rolled his eyes. "I tried to tell her they're wild and free all over Waterford, but she'd have no part of letting it go. We now have a bunny."

"I thought Christian would like him," Chloe said. "But we didn't see the dog anywhere. Sorry."

Daniel managed not to react with how wretched he felt. Little Jack Frost was out there, running around, not frozen, not in the lake, not lost in the woods. "Maybe Liam or Garrett found him. Go show Christian his new pet."

"That he will promptly put back in the wild tomorrow," Shane added.

"When that raccoon is not around," Chloe said.

Shane sighed. "Fine. Don't we have a bunny cage down in the ATV shed, Dad? I could have sworn we had one."

"Sure do."

"I'll get it," Shane said. "You go tell Christian he now has Saint Nick, the Christmas bunny."

Daniel gave a soft laugh as they went off, standing sentry at the door again, waiting for the rest of his family to return. Behind him, he heard the occasional bout of laughter and chatter from the living room, the bark of a dog, and Christian's squeal of delight.

From the driveway, he saw a flashlight moving quickly as if being carried by someone running, then stopping and…kissing.

He caught a glimpse of reddish-blond hair and knew it was Garrett and Jessie, who looked very happy to be together, but didn't have a dog with them. He watched them walk and stop and kiss again, a little more desperate than he'd expect after hunting for a lost dog on Christmas Eve. More like one of them had been lost and then found.

Garrett put his hand on Jessie's face and stroked her cheek, saying something that made her laugh and wrap her arms around his neck for another kiss. Daniel told himself he shouldn't watch, but he couldn't stop, remembering those years with Annie, when kissing was all they ever wanted to do.

"I'm doing my best," he whispered to his absent wife. "I got Jessie to stay when Garrett wanted her to leave. Put Shane and Chloe on the same project. Steered Liam back to Andi. I'm working on all of them, Annie girl."

No one answered him, of course, but the young couple in the drive finally tore themselves apart and came to the kitchen door.

"No luck?" he asked as he let them in.

"Forget the lost dog," Jessie said, dropping her head on Garrett's shoulder. "I nearly lost a man."

Daniel drew back from his son, blinking in surprise. "You got lost in the southern woods? You know that area like the back of your hand."

"Well, apparently my hand was all turned around," Garrett said sheepishly. "But..." He gave Jessie a smile. "Someone braved the dark and found me." He nuzzled her closer, their down jackets scratching against each other. "Found me and saved me."

"Oh boy." Jessie smiled, but rolled her eyes at Daniel. "He's making it sound more dramatic than it was. I had a flashlight and a big mouth. But I'm really sorry we didn't find the dog, Dr. K."

"Well, thanks to both of you for looking." He helped Jessie out of her jacket and whispered, "You earned a Jameson's before church."

"At least one." She laughed, putting her arm around Garrett to head into the living room, leaving Daniel to look for one more son.

Why hadn't Liam called? He took out his own phone, but didn't see a message or missed call.

"Everyone but Liam and Andi?" Gramma Finnie asked, joining him in the kitchen.

"Did you talk to him or get a response to your text?" Daniel asked.

She shook her head, but both of them turned at the sound of a dog barking. Gramma gasped softly, echoing the skip of Daniel's heart. Was that...

Jag came bounding forward, barking furiously. Daniel threw open the door just as Shane came up from the shed, dragging a rabbit cage.

"Where's Liam?" Shane asked.

"He's not answering my texts," Gramma said.

Jag barked again and again, bringing everyone from the living room.

"He's pulling a Lassie," Garrett suggested.

Daniel nodded in full agreement. "He knows where Liam is."

"Let's go!"

In seconds, his sons and nephews poured out of the house, not one of them bothering to stop for a jacket, though a few grabbed flashlights. All of them followed Jag into the night, this time on a hunt for their missing brother.

"What the hell else could go wrong?" Daniel whispered to Gramma Finnie. "They say trouble comes in threes."

"Irish don't say that." She handed him a shot glass. "We say the best is yet to come."

If only that were true, Daniel thought, tossing back the shot. If only the best days weren't behind him.

Chapter Seven

When his mother announced that they were skipping Midnight Mass, Daniel not only took that as "number three" of things that could go wrong, he considered it might be the actual apocalypse.

No one argued with the decision, that was for sure. It had been late by the time the boys returned with Liam on an ATV. Another half hour had passed while his brothers ribbed him for his monumental stupidity. Then Molly wrapped Liam's sprained ankle, doing the job so slowly, Daniel wondered if it wasn't her way of guaranteeing they all got out of Mass.

Truth was, the whole evening seemed off, but none of the kids appeared to mind a bit. They were cheery, with that buzz of anticipation that Daniel remembered from years gone by.

Of course, the eggnog and whiskey had flowed a little heavier than usual, which seemed to do the trick to wipe away the undercurrent of sadness over the lost dog.

He tried to shake off his blues as they started the gift exchange. They were about halfway through when

Gramma Finnie stood up from her chair and slapped her hands against weathered cheeks.

"We forgot to light the candle!"

That got a huge and mixed response from the crowd.

"Uh, we didn't exactly forget, Gramma," Molly said on a guilty laugh.

"We're lit enough," Darcy joked.

"Just do the short version, please," Shane said. "I'm about to reveal the best bad T-shirts ever given to dog trainers."

Gramma silenced them all with a look. "Tradition is tradition, and this one is forever."

"And it *takes* forever," Shane added.

More moans and groans followed, but Garrett got up and found the long lighter and made a show of handing it to her with a bow. "For the lighting of the candle, madam."

"Thank you, lad," she said. "You're the best in the bunch."

That had earned the expected response from his brothers and cousins and more laughter from everyone. Daniel sat perched on the arm of a chair next to the fire, able to see out the front window on the off chance that...

No, he had to stop. Talk about stupidity. What could be worse than silently praying your deceased wife would work a miracle to bring home a lost dog? He forced his gaze off the outdoors and onto his dear, sweet mother, who took her long lighter and stood in front of the lantern and candle.

"In the south of Ireland, near the County Waterford, where we get our glorious name and heritage, there is a tradition that began in the seventeenth century…" She leaned close to Christian, who was watching, rapt. "When the Catholics were suppressed."

He blinked his little-boy eyes at her, confused but mesmerized.

"By lighting the candle, the people were signaling to any passing priests that the family inside was Catholic."

"Unless they skipped Midnight Mass," Molly whispered.

"Then they were just sinners," Liam replied, both of them getting dark looks from Gramma, who took her heritage seriously.

"But that drew the attention of English soldiers!" Gramma said, adding a flair for the dramatic that ran in her bloodline.

Daniel only half listened, enjoying the lilt of his mother's brogue, taken back to when he was the child in this room, then the young husband, then a proud father, and now…a grandfather. So many Christmases come and gone at Waterford Farm. Fifty-nine of them.

"How did that happen?" Christian's question echoed the one in Daniel's head.

"Oh, I'm so glad you asked, lad."

"Coal for you, little man," Shane joked. "'Cause now we're definitely getting the long version."

"I like your stories, Gramma Finnie," Christian said, earning a beaming smile from the old woman in front of him.

"And you are a mighty good addition to the clan, lad. Maybe your fine uncles can learn from your interest."

Everyone laughed, and when that died down, Gramma continued.

"Yes, they told the soldiers that the lights were to guide Mary and Joseph along the way to the stable to bring in baby Jesus, and the soldiers fell for it!"

"Just like Liam down that hill," Garrett said in a stage whisper, veering them all back into laughter and away from the story.

"It'll just take me longer if you keep interrupting," Gramma warned, her blue eyes dancing with affection, because complaining about the story was as much a tradition as lighting the actual candle.

"But what about the soldiers, Gramma?" Christian asked, oblivious to the family dynamic and caught up in a new Christmas story.

"Well, the soldiers believed them, and the tradition continued. To this very day, the candle is lit in every Irish home to welcome anyone who might be passing by, needing some food, or lonely and lost on Christmas." She snapped the lighter and held it over the candle, glancing out the window. "So that's why we light one right here in the Kilcannon home, in case—"

She looked up just as the candle lit, her jaw dropping.

"Did you hear that?" she said in a hushed tone.

"A dog?"

"I heard a bark!"

"Definitely a dog!"

Half of them were up, but somehow Daniel beat them all to the front door, a little ashamed of how badly he wanted Jack Frost to be trotting up the walkway.

He yanked open the door to a gust of cold air,

blinking at the silhouette of a man coming into the light of the house. A big man, muscular, with his heavy-jacketed arms wrapped around something small and tan and definitely barking.

But it wasn't the dog that made Daniel Kilcannon's heart stop beating in his chest. It wasn't the miracle that made Gramma Finnie murmur an Irish prayer of gratitude. It wasn't the impossibly perfect timing that made every single Kilcannon in the room stand in shocked silence behind him.

It was the blue eyes, golden hair, and irrepressible smile of a soldier they missed more than they could express.

"I found this little guy wandering around." Aidan walked in and offered the dog to Molly, who stood next to Daniel with tears already streaming.

"Son." Daniel could barely say the word as he embraced his youngest boy and squeezed his strong, healthy, so very much alive body. "You're home." His voice cracked, but he didn't care.

"I got leave for the holidays." Aidan hugged back, hard enough to damn near fracture a rib, but Daniel didn't care. "Don't tell me I missed the Christmas candle story!"

In the outburst of hoots, hollers, hugs, and dances of disbelief, Daniel inched away and drank in the high fives, the tears, the squeals of delight, and an insane amount of barking.

The room was bursting at its seams as Daniel tried to get his bearings. Weight and sadness and grief and disappointment lifted from his shoulders, leaving him unbalanced with nothing but pure joy. The deepest, most profound joy he'd felt in years.

His gaze moved around the faces of his family as they looked at him, their beaming smiles, some tears, a lot of laughs, and that familial sense of…of…*holy hell.*

"You knew." He could barely say the words, taking in Shane's victorious grin and Garrett's satisfied nod and Molly's smug expression of a person who'd successfully pulled off a surprise. "You *all* knew."

"Not all of us!" Pru squealed, visibly torn between the joy of a surprise and not being in on it.

"You'd have put Aidan on the calendar," Liam teased. "Couldn't risk the security breach."

"I didn't know," Chloe said.

"Nor I," Jessie chimed in, looking at Andi.

"I fell harder than my husband down that hill," she replied.

All three women looked at their respective men, who looked at each other like they wanted someone else to answer.

"It was a group decision to keep you in the dark," Liam finally said. "We thought the fewer people who knew the better."

"When you insisted on going, we just kind of silently agreed we'd pretend to be looking for the dog," Garrett said, hugging Jessie tighter. "Don't be mad."

"You sure it wasn't a test?" Chloe asked. "To see if we are 'real' Kilcannons?"

"Based on the bunny save, you passed," Shane joked.

"Speaking of 'real.'" Daniel pointed to Liam's injured ankle. "Is that?"

"Sadly, it is," Liam said sheepishly. "Got a little carried away trying to convince my wife I really was worried about that dog."

"I think we all did," Garrett said on a laugh.

"But where was the dog?" Daniel asked as he reached to take Jack Frost from Ella's hands, where he was being well loved.

"He's been in the kennels sound asleep all evening," Darcy assured him. "When the fire department called this afternoon, I thought of the whole plan."

"Wasn't my acting amazing?" Ella asked as she relinquished the pup.

"We literally had no idea how we were going to drag things out and skip Midnight Mass so we could be here, at home, when Aidan arrived," Shane said. "But then Jack Frost gave us the perfect story."

"It takes a village to fool the father." Aidan grinned at Daniel. "And we knew it would take an act of God for Gramma to skip Midnight Mass."

Gramma Finnie gave a smug smile. "I agreed to the plan without question when I heard it."

"*You* knew?" Daniel nearly choked.

"Only after you left. Darcy came back to the house and whispered the truth to me, so I could time the lighting of the candle for Aidan's arrival."

"Aidan's your Christmas surprise from all of us," Molly said, sliding her arm around Daniel. "Are you happy, Dad? It's all we really wanted this year."

Happy? He couldn't speak or breathe. "I just..." Damn the tears. He blinked them back and looked at Aidan, dressed in camos, a true warrior who probably moved heaven and earth to get this leave.

"Hey." Aidan took a step closer and put his hand on Daniel's shoulder. "This was all my idea. You can't be the only one pulling strings to make things happen, Dogfather."

Daniel hugged his youngest son again, making the dog bark and the family cheer. Over Aidan's mighty shoulder, he let his gaze skim the red and gold ribbons, sparkling white lights, and a roaring fire of comfort, until it landed on the tree.

There, he found a picture of a smiling young bride, looking right at him, promising to never leave his side.

Merry Christmas, Annie girl.

And for the first time since the day he said goodbye to her, he felt the tiniest, most infinitesimal stirring of something in his soul. Hope.

That was Annie's gift this year, the best gift of all.

If you want to stay up-to-date on every release, sign up for my newsletter.

www.roxannestclaire.com/newsletter-2/

And join the private Facebook group of Dogfather fans for inside scoop, secret tidbits, and fun giveaways!

www.facebook.com/groups/roxannestclairereaders/

I answer all messages and emails personally, so don't hesitate to write to roxanne@roxannestclaire.com!

Fall In Love With
The Dogfather Series...

Sign up for the newsletter for the next release date!

www.roxannestclaire.com/newsletter/

Available Now

SIT...STAY...BEG (Book 1)

NEW LEASH ON LIFE (Book 2)

LEADER OF THE PACK (Book 3)

SANTA PAWS IS COMING TO TOWN (Book 4)
(A Holiday Novella)

BAD TO THE BONE (Book 5)

RUFF AROUND THE EDGES (Book 6)

DOUBLE DOG DARE (Book 7)

BARK! THE HERALD ANGELS SING (Book 8)
(A Holiday Novella)

Coming Next

OLD DOG NEW TRICKS (Book 9)

THE
Barefoot Bay
SERIES

Welcome to Barefoot Bay! On these sun-washed shores you'll meet heroes who'll steal your heart, heroines who'll make you stand up and cheer, and characters who quickly become familiar and beloved. Some are spicy, some are sweet, but every book in the Barefoot Bay series stands alone, and tempts readers to come back again and again. So, kick off your shoes and fall in love with billionaires, brides, bodyguards, silver foxes, and more...all on one dreamy island.

THE BAREFOOT BAY SERIES

1 – Secrets on the Sand

2 – Seduction on the Sand

3 – Scandal on the Sand

4 – Barefoot in White

5 – Barefoot in Lace

6 – Barefoot in Pearls

7 – Barefoot Bound (*novella*)

8 – Barefoot with a Bodyguard

9 – Barefoot with a Stranger

10 – Barefoot with a Bad Boy

11 – Barefoot Dreams (*novella*)

12 – Barefoot at Sunset

13 – Barefoot at Moonrise

14 – Barefoot at Midnight

Want to know the day the next Roxanne St. Claire book is released? Sign up for the newsletter! You'll get brief monthly e-mails about new releases and book sales.

www.roxannestclaire.com/newsletter.html

About The Author

Published since 2003, Roxanne St. Claire is a *New York Times* and *USA Today* bestselling author of more than fifty romance and suspense novels. She has written several popular series, including The Dogfather, Barefoot Bay, the Guardian Angelinos, and the Bullet Catchers.

In addition to being a ten-time nominee and one-time winner of the prestigious RITA™ Award for the best in romance writing, Roxanne has won the National Readers' Choice Award for best romantic suspense three times, as well as the Maggie, the Daphne du Maurier Award, the HOLT Medallion, Booksellers' Best, Book Buyers Best, the Award of Excellence, and many others.

She lives in Florida with her husband, and still attempts to run the lives of her young adult children. She loves dogs, books, chocolate, and wine, especially all at the same time.

www.roxannestclaire.com
www.twitter.com/roxannestclaire
www.facebook.com/roxannestclaire
www.roxannestclaire.com/newsletter/

14704669R00149

Made in the USA
Middletown, DE
20 November 2018